'You're only _____
should be living _____

Wasn't she? Over the _____
she'd had the best of both worlds. She'd
enjoyed her work and she'd been out with the
occasional man, but for her daughter's sake
she'd finished any relationship when it had
started to get serious.

'Shouldn't you?' Liam prompted with a
frown.

Realising he expected an answer, Bea tried to
recall what the question had been. But for the
life of her she couldn't. Apart from the fact
that it had made her angry. 'Shouldn't I
what?'

He attempted valiantly to hide his exasperation, but she could read it plainly in his
eyes. 'Be enjoying life to the full.'

Although a Lancastrian by birth, **Sheila Danton** has now settled in the West Country with her husband. Her nursing career, which took her to many parts of England, left her with 'itchy feet', which she indulges by travelling both at home and abroad. She uses her trips to discover new settings for her books, and also to visit her three grown-up children, who have flown the nest in different directions.

Recent titles by the same author:

GOOD HUSBAND MATERIAL

THE PATIENT LOVER

BY
SHEILA DANTON

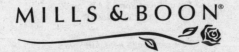

MILLS & BOON®

DID YOU PURCHASE THIS BOOK WITHOUT A COVER?

If you did, you should be aware it is **stolen property** as it was reported *unsold and destroyed* by a retailer. Neither the author nor the publisher has received any payment for this book.

All the characters in this book have no existence outside the imagination of the author, and have no relation whatsoever to anyone bearing the same name or names. They are not even distantly inspired by any individual known or unknown to the author, and all the incidents are pure invention.

All Rights Reserved including the right of reproduction in whole or in part in any form. This edition is published by arrangement with Harlequin Enterprises II B.V. The text of this publication or any part thereof may not be reproduced or transmitted in any form or by any means, electronic or mechanical, including photocopying, recording, storage in an information retrieval system, or otherwise, without the written permission of the publisher.

This book is sold subject to the condition that it shall not, by way of trade or otherwise, be lent, resold, hired out or otherwise circulated without the prior consent of the publisher in any form of binding or cover other than that in which it is published and without a similar condition including this condition being imposed on the subsequent purchaser.

MILLS & BOON and MILLS & BOON with the Rose Device are registered trademarks of the publisher.

First published in Great Britain 2001
Harlequin Mills & Boon Limited,
Eton House, 18-24 Paradise Road, Richmond, Surrey TW9 1SR

© Sheila Danton 2001

ISBN 0 263 82283 4

Set in Times Roman 10½ on 12 pt.
03-0101-46648

Printed and bound in Spain
by Litografía Rosés, S.A., Barcelona

CHAPTER ONE

BEA SETON waited anxiously in the waiting room of the health centre for her daughter to show up. She'd gone to a lot of trouble to arrange for Ruth to work as a temporary receptionist until she went to university, and it looked as if she was about to be let down on the first day. How could her daughter, on whom she had lavished such care and training, behave so thoughtlessly?

The door banged open and, as if pursued by the unseasonably ferocious wind, Ruth bounded in. She was followed by a man who Bea presumed was a patient, his smartly groomed appearance somewhat dishevelled by the weather.

'You're late,' she admonished Ruth, who merely grinned and disappeared into the manager's office.

'I'm so sorry. I know it sounds ridiculous in July, but the road was blocked by a fallen tree.'

Bea swung round as she heard the stranger replying to her accusation. 'Oh! I wasn't—I didn't...'

Her intention to disclaim any knowledge of him was cut short as she met the disarming grin of a good-looking and confident male, not as middle-aged as she had first thought. He had smoothed down his wind-blown dark hair, and was surveying her with eyes of an incredible startling blue.

'I—I was actually talking to my daughter, not you. Who was it you wanted to see?'

He ignored her question and frowned. 'Your daughter? You're not trying to tell me that was your daughter who rescued me in the car park?'

Here we go again, Bea thought wearily. 'I'm afraid I am. And, yes, I was very young when she was born and, yes, she looks older than she really is.'

His grin widened. 'I can see I'm not the first to ask that and I apologise. It was very rude of me.'

Bea inclined her head in acknowledgement and asked, 'Do you have an appointment?'

'I told your practice manager I'd be here following morning surgery. I guess she won't be too pleased to see me at lunchtime.'

Bea understood then. Mair Banks, the practice manager, usually arranged for drug reps to come at that time.

'She's actually just back from her lunch-break, but my daughter is closeted with her at the moment. I'm the practice nurse, by the way, and I'm afraid there aren't any doctors here at the moment.'

'There's one,' he told her with a broad smile that revealed his even white teeth.

She looked around with a frown, and then realised her mistake as he said, 'I'm Dr Taylor, Liam Taylor.' He proffered a hand in her direction.

She groaned and grasped his hand warmly. 'You're the locum due to start tomorrow?'

'Afraid so,' he told her with a pretence at humility.

'W-welcome to B-Bargate,' she stuttered, trying to ignore her body's reaction to his strong handshake. 'I'll let Mrs Banks know you're here.'

He released her hand reluctantly. 'If you must. But I'm quite happy talking to you.'

'Maybe, but my first afternoon appointment will be here at any moment.' Although aware that he was an unattached male, Bea ignored the hint of suggestion in his remark. She had no intention of going down that route.

He nodded, and as she started to move away he checked her identity badge and murmured quietly, 'Pleased to have met you, Sister B. Seton.'

'Beatrice Seton,' she told him, 'commonly known as Bea.'

Her cheeks coloured as he replied, 'A beautiful name for a beautiful person.'

She knocked sharply on Mair's door and, without waiting for an answer, marched in. 'Dr Liam Taylor is here to see you. His journey was delayed by a fallen tree.'

Mair looked up at Bea in surprise, and Bea was conscious that her response to Liam Taylor's compliment must still be visible on her face. 'Ruth has already told me the story. I'm just on my way out to see him.'

While she'd been talking, Bea had noticed Ruth escape and take up her position on the reception desk. Hopefully she would take note of all Bargate Health Centre's most experienced employee, Katy, could teach her.

When Bea went out to collect her first patient, she experienced a pinprick of resentment at the sight of Alicia, the practice's only unmarried partner, finding the time to listen rapturously to a story recounted by Liam.

Although, as she led Mrs Parton into the treatment room for her weekly weigh-in and pep talk, she had to concede it wasn't surprising. Liam Taylor had everything. Startling good looks, a seductive voice and firm muscles rippling under an expensively cut dark suit. And, she supposed, brains.

She started on her afternoon list with the oddest of

sensations fluttering in her stomach. A feeling which she uncomfortably tried to dissect during her teabreak. Surely she didn't consider she had a proprietary interest in Liam just because she'd been the first to greet him and he'd said nice things about her? Even if she was already in a committed relationship, Alicia had just as much right to chat with him as she had.

No, it was more likely that she was unsettled because Ruth, starting her vacation job that afternoon, was making her realise just how soon her daughter would leave her on her own for the first time in eighteen years. Coping with Ruth growing up might have been hard at times, but it had also been fun. Great fun. So there was no doubt she would miss her.

'Your three-thirty appointment has arrived, Sister Seton.'

Ruth's voice broke in on her reverie and Bea smiled at her daughter's professionalism. 'Thank *you*, Miss Seton. I'll be with her in a moment.'

Cilla Jenkins had barely closed the door behind her when she burst into tears. Bea led her to a chair and placed a box of tissues within reach.

'What's the problem?' she asked the sixteen-year-old.

'My boyfriend's condom split on Saturday night and my mum'll kill me if I get pregnant.'

Bea placed a supportive hand on the girl's shoulder. She waited for the outburst of weeping to begin to subside, then said quietly, 'We can do something to help you, if it's necessary. First I need to ask you a few questions so that we can decide if it is.'

'The morning-after pill, you mean? Isn't it too late for that?'

'That's the name it's known by but it should really

be called the 72-hour-after pill. It works if taken any time up to three days after unprotected sex.'

Cilla looked up at her with wide, scared eyes. 'You mean...' Hardly daring to voice her hopes, she didn't finish the sentence.

'I mean it's a possibility, but before we make any decisions I need a few answers and to do some routine health checks.'

The young girl scrubbed at her eyes with a tissue and gulped in a lungful of air. 'Right. What do you want to know?'

Bea gave her an encouraging smile. 'First of all, exactly what happened?'

Cilla was so embarrassed that her description was sketchy in the extreme, but Bea decided not to press her for more details at that moment. 'Next, I need to know if your menstrual cycle is regular?'

The girl nodded.

'Every twenty-eight days?'

Another nod.

'And where are you in your cycle at the moment?'

Cilla frowned and Bea pushed a calendar over to her. After a few moments of frantic reckoning, she settled on a date.

Bea gave her a wry smile. 'Your most fertile time, I'm afraid, so we do need to consider post-coital contraception this time.'

When Cilla nodded but didn't speak, Bea cautioned, 'The four tablets used for this are a very high dose of the ordinary contraceptive Pill, so it should only be used in emergencies and should certainly not be used repeatedly. Have you ever taken it before?'

Cilla shook her head.

'Or been on the Pill?'

Another silent shake of the head.

'I now need to ask you some questions about your general health and that of your family, and then I want you to tell me again exactly what happened.'

More confident now, the girl had soon said enough to persuade Bea there was a definite need for the treatment but she had to make sure that there were no obvious contraindications.

Her gentle physical examination was completed by checking the girl's blood pressure.

'Everything's fine, so I think we can go ahead with the prescription, but first there are a few points I need to make.'

When she'd finished, she checked her watch. 'Dr Jones should be in soon for an afternoon clinic. I'll just ask the receptionist to tell her I need to see her.'

She closed the door behind her and saw Alicia Jones again conversing with Liam Taylor. She felt another momentary stab of resentment that Alicia could find so much time to chat.

It was something she found difficult to understand, because she loved her work and had never been one for standing about gossiping, but, then, it had been a long time since she'd come across a man quite so seductively attractive as their new doctor. Since...well, since that disastrous and short-lived relationship with Gary, she supposed.

Dismissing such ridiculous thoughts, she strode across to join them and said, 'Could I have a word with you, Alicia, before you start on the antenatals? It's about a patient.' She gestured to the room where Cilla was waiting.

'Sure.' Alicia swung round, causing her shoulder-length blonde hair to swing out and brush Liam's cheek.

'Come across to my room. Anything Liam shouldn't hear?'

'I guess not if he's going to be working here.'

They made their way into Alicia's room and Bea described Cilla's problem.

'So she needs a prescription for PC4?' Alicia asked, already pulling her prescription pad towards her. 'Have you explained its dangers to her?'

'I did, but she was in such a state I'm not sure how much she took in. I intend to reinforce everything I've said when I give her the prescription, and make sure she keeps the follow-up appointments I give her.'

Liam nodded. 'Would you like me to see her? I know I'm not officially on duty today, but this is something I feel quite strongly about. Now these pills are so much more readily available at some clinics, it's important for her to understand the danger of relying on this form of contraception.'

'I've already emphasised that.' Stung by his apparent criticism, Bea looked to Alicia for her support, but she was already nodding and smiling appreciatively. 'That would be great. It's important for a doctor to deal with these cases and, anyway, I expect there are other patients waiting for the nurse's attention.'

Aghast, Bea couldn't believe Alicia was referring to her so dismissively.

'I'm going to look up some notes now, so you can use my room.' Alicia bounded to her feet. 'Perhaps you'd bring Cilla and her notes across for Dr Taylor, Bea.'

Hardly able to believe what was happening, Bea bit back the retort hovering on her lips. In her time at the health centre, Alicia had never asked to see the patient herself but had accepted that Bea knew what she was doing and had done everything necessary. This departure was obviously for Liam's benefit! Because Alicia was jealous of her earlier exchange with him perhaps?

She had always had a good rapport with all the doctors, and her work had never been questioned. So how could the arrival of one attractive man on the scene cause such a change? Not only in Alicia, but in herself. Hadn't Bea experienced antagonism towards Alicia because she'd been chatting with him while she'd been working?

Or was the change in herself purely down to the empty-nest syndrome? Was the first day of Ruth's holiday job making her over-sensitive?

She tried to dismiss her uneasiness as she returned to the treatment room. 'Dr Taylor will see you now and give you the prescription.'

'Dr Taylor?' Cilla frowned.

'He's new to the practice. Very approachable. I'll take you across to him.'

She did so and called in her next patient, determinedly pushing distracting thoughts of Liam Taylor to the back of her mind.

The remainder of her afternoon list was uneventful, allowing her to finish on time.

She waited until Ruth was free and, handing over the notes from the session she had just completed, told her, 'I'll see you later. Do you want me to come and collect you?'

'Mum! I'm eighteen, not eight.' A patient approaching the desk allowed her to escape. 'I must get back to work. See you later.'

Although she hadn't eaten anything since breakfast and was hungry herself, Bea delayed their evening meal until Ruth finally arrived home.

'How did you get on today?' she asked as she served out the chicken casserole.

'It was great. I can see why you enjoy working there.'

'Did you meet all of the doctors?'

'All but John Adams. But, then, I've always known him.'

'Of course, he wouldn't have been in today. As senior partner he now has Mondays off. Gives him a long weekend.'

Ruth looked down at the empty mug in her hand. 'I must say, they were all very nice to me, especially that new chap. Until Dr Jones swept him off downtown for a meal.'

Although not believing it herself, Bea said, 'She's probably showing him our catchment area in case he has any urgent visits to make.'

'Huh! I don't think so for one moment. She's not let him out of her sight all afternoon. I'd say she's got the hots for him.'

'Ruth!'

Bea's horrified reprimand went unheeded as Ruth continued, 'You should have seen her—I gather she's unattached?'

'She's not married, certainly, but she does have a partner.'

'Well, the way she was going on this afternoon she's obviously not getting what she needs from him.'

'Ruth!' Bea admonished again. 'You musn't say such things, especially about one of the doctors.'

'Why not? I'm only repeating what the other girls are saying.'

Bea was about to retort that a daughter of hers should know better than to repeat gossip when she checked herself.

Ruth was old enough to be responsible for her own behaviour, and if she didn't know what was right and wrong by now, it was surely Bea's fault. In trying not to impose the restrictions on Ruth that had made her own early life so miserable, had she been *too* lenient?

How could a parent ever know if they were doing it right? Being too strict, as her own parents had been, had resulted in her rebelling and spending the night with Gary— At the time it had seemed preferable to facing up to her father's anger at her breaking his ten p.m. curfew.

Being too lenient, as perhaps she herself had been, had led to Ruth having no qualms about saying exactly what she thought. Or was this just how teenage girls gossiped these days when they were together?

If so, any show of disapproval would make life at the health centre impossible for Ruth. Perhaps it had been a mistake to arrange for them to work together?

Clearly sensing Bea's unspoken censure, Ruth shrugged, then hungrily finished her evening meal. Immediately collecting up both their plates, she said, 'I'm not used to working so late. Do you mind if I go to bed early?'

Aware that working together, as well as living together, was not going to be as easy as she had thought, Bea offered diffidently, 'I'll be leaving at eight in the morning if you want a lift.' If her daughter preferred to be independent, that was all right by her.

Ruth's mind was clearly too full of the day's events to think about travel arrangements. 'It'll be interesting to see how Liam enjoys being a toy boy. Goodnight, Mum.'

Toy boy? Was that how the health centre gossips were already referring to Alicia and Liam? She didn't exactly remember his age but, having read on his CV the number of posts he'd held, she thought he must be approaching forty. At least. Perhaps he *was* a little young for Alicia, but just the right age for her.

Now, where had that thought come from? What charisma the man must have! To have that effect on her when for all these years while she had been raising Ruth she hadn't given any man a second thought. One thing was for sure. She wasn't going to let him know it. Unlike Alicia, she would keep such a strict control on her emotions that he would never know just how aware of him she was.

As she prepared for bed, Bea thought again about the decisions she had had to make over the years.

Her own mother and father had only done what they'd thought right and, though they had thrown her out when they'd known she'd been pregnant, Bea was glad her repeated approaches had eventually led to a reconciliation.

It was a pity her parents hadn't enjoyed Ruth in her early days, but she was an accepted member of the family now, more so than Bea. And she guessed this was partly her fault. Despite her determination that Ruth should know her grandparents, she supposed she herself still harboured resentment at them not supporting her in her time of need.

How different it could have been. Advice would have been available, as it was for Cilla, but such things had never been discussed in her home and, having been the original innocent abroad, she hadn't thought about looking for it until she'd been on her own and had needed help.

It had been too late then. Not that she regretted Ruth's birth for one moment. She had brought so much happiness into Bea's life. But the experience had made her determined that Ruth should know the facts of life from an early age and, if possible, she herself would learn how to help others in a similar predicament.

She hadn't been able to start her nurse training until Ruth had been at school, but the sacrifice had been worth it. She loved her work.

Bea was leaving the house at eight the next morning when Ruth came tumbling down the stairs, dressed but with dishevelled hair, no make-up and eyes that were barely open. Without a word, she climbed into the passenger seat of the car and pulled down the sun visor to see herself in the mirror.

With a groan, she rummaged through her bag and found a comb and some basic make-up. Still without speaking, she proceeded to try and rectify the ravages of the night.

'Did you oversleep?' Bea asked.

'I heard my alarm but went back to sleep.'

'Help yourself to anything you need from my bag.'

Ruth turned and grinned at her. 'Thanks, Mum. I don't need as much camouflage as you!'

Bea nodded affectionately. This was more like the old Ruth.

While she was locking the car her daughter raced into the health centre, and by the time Bea followed she was already at work behind the desk.

A feeling of satisfaction washed over Bea and her worries of the night before drained away as she started on her morning's list.

Ruth came into the treatment room when Bea was snatching a quick coffee-break. 'Between your appointments Liam would like you to see this patient of his. He needs a dressing done.'

Bea frowned. 'Did he say what kind of dressing?'

'It's all in here.' She handed over the patient's notes.

'I'm not sure when I can fit him in. I've a pretty full list already.'

'I know, but Liam said he knew *you'd* manage to do it.'

Torn between pleasure that he must think her competent and her determination not to allow his flattery to turn her head, she muttered, 'OK, I'll see my next appointment now and then try and squeeze Mr Darby in.'

Her next patient wasn't one to be hurried. Sharon Gimby had too many problems. She had been injured by a terrorist bomb in London several years before, and although the physical scars had healed the resulting facial disfigurement and mental scars had left her unable to cope with life. She had returned to the family home, looking for comfort and security, and almost immediately her father had suffered a stroke. The worry had precipitated her mother into the early stages of Alzheimer's disease, leaving Sharon to assume responsibility for them both.

Now she was in her late fifties, living alone and undergoing radiotherapy following removal of a breast lump.

'What can I do for you today, Sharon?'

'I fell on Sunday and hurt my arm.'

'Which one?'

She pointed to her right arm.

'What happened?'

Sharon haltingly described how she had slipped in the kitchen and bumped her arm on the work surface.

Bea examined the arm and tried to discover exactly

where it hurt. She could see a bruise, but as Sharon kept changing her mind about where it was paining her she guessed it was just one more cry for help.

After thoroughly examining the area and making sure Sharon could move the arm freely, she smiled and said reassuringly, 'I think you've knocked it rather hard, but I can't find any sign of serious injury.'

Sharon's face fell at the consultation being over, but brightened immediately as Bea continued, 'What does worry me, though, is why you slipped. What kind of flooring do you have in the kitchen?'

'It has a pattern on it.'

'Not carpet?'

She shook her head. 'It's shiny.'

'Tiles?'

Again Sharon shook her head. 'Not tiles. There's no cracks. I don't know what it's made of.'

Bea presumed it was a type of cushion flooring, unless it was ancient linoleum.

'So are you careful to wipe up any spills as soon as they happen?'

Sharon looked blank.

'If you spill water or fat, do you clean it up immediately?'

'If I notice. The home help washes the floor.'

'How often does Mrs Bell come in?'

'Once a week.'

Bea knew Mrs Bell was Sharon's only human contact, apart from her visits to the health centre and the hospital. The social worker attached to the practice was trying to find a place for her at a day centre, but there weren't enough to go round and Sharon was considered fit enough to get out and about on her own.

But she shunned contact with anyone who didn't

know her and so never ventured anywhere she hadn't been before. Her home care assistant had to do all her shopping.

'You must try and keep it clean and dry in between, otherwise one day you're going to hurt yourself badly.'

'I know. Everything's just such an effort at the moment, though.' Bea saw her patient's eyes fill with tears and rested her hand over her arm.

'You do very well, Sharon.' Bea checked her watch. 'What are you doing later this morning?'

She sniffed. 'Going home.'

'Why not potter around the shops for a while and then come back for a chat at the end of my list? Say about twelve-fifteen?'

'I don't need any shopping.'

'Just window-shop, then. You won't need to speak to anyone. Do you think you could manage that?'

'Suppose so.' Sharon nodded and plodded towards the door.

'See you later.'

Bea sighed and followed her out to call in Liam's patient. 'Come through, Mr Darby.'

She seated him on the treatment chair and gave him a welcoming smile. 'Sorry to have kept you waiting.' She washed her hands and removed the old dressing Liam had temporarily reapplied to a burn on his patient's arm.

She bit back a gasp of horror when she saw it. 'Hmm. This could do with cleaning up a bit. When did you do it?'

Bea checked Liam's instructions on the record card and decided to ignore them. For one thing she didn't have the dressings he had prescribed, and even if she had, she didn't consider they were right for Mr Darby's wound.

She cleaned it up thoroughly and dressed it firmly while he told her all about his accident when the car had overheated.

'I didn't think, see. I wanted to put more water in and the steam was ferocious. I don't think I've ever known such pain.'

'I can imagine. There, that should feel better,' she told him eventually.

Mr Darby smiled. 'It feels wonderful. Whatever you've put on it is so soothing. Thanks a lot, Sister.'

'I'd like to see you again tomorrow. Make an appointment on the way out, would you?'

Mr Darby smiled and left her. Bea noted down her actions and put the notes aside to discuss with Liam Taylor at the earliest opportunity. Which probably wouldn't be until much later as her list was already running late and she had Sharon coming back for a chat during her lunch hour.

The remainder of the morning was filled with injections, ear-syringing and taking blood. When her last patient had left, she realised her restless night was catching up on her and decided to have a quick coffee and eat the sandwich she had brought with her before she saw Sharon.

While the kettle boiled she popped out to Reception and asked if Liam was free, but he had already left to do some visits.

'Right, Katy. Thanks.' She looked round and, finding no sign of Ruth, said, 'Is my daughter shaping up all right?'

Katy smiled. 'She's a great help. She's just popped

out for a sandwich and has taken orders from the rest of us. Didn't she ask you what you wanted?'

'She knew I always bring my own.' Bea didn't let on that she'd also made one for Ruth.

Bea returned to her room, wondering when shopping had become part of a receptionist's duties. As if she didn't know! Ruth could be impossibly persuasive when there was something she wanted, and she had clearly wanted to get out to the shops.

She closed the treatment room door and sighed, before wading into a mound of outstanding paperwork. She'd barely started when Katy rang through to say that Sharon was there early to see her.

It was clearly going to be one of those days!

She made coffee for them both and offered Sharon Ruth's sandwich. When it was refused, she reluctantly forewent her own and settled to chat until it was time for Sharon to leave for her radiotherapy appointment.

Bea's first afternoon patient had arrived by that time so she resigned herself to going without her lunch break that day.

CHAPTER TWO

LATER in the afternoon Ruth brought in an apology for non-arrival from Bea's next patient.

'Thanks for this. It'll give me a chance to eat my sandwich. I'm starving. I've not had a long enough break between patients until now.' Bea looked up from pouring boiling water in her cup and enquired, 'Tea?'

Ruth shook her head. 'I'd better get back and see if Katy needs me. But before I go, I thought you'd like to hear what they're saying about Liam now.'

She was obviously bursting to share the gossip that was circulating amongst the reception staff but, not wanting to encourage it, Bea said, 'I'm not sure that I want to.'

Ruth gave her no choice. 'Apparently he's going abroad to get over a disastrous relationship and he travels light because she cleaned him out.'

'Who says?'

'Well, Katy told me but I suppose Alicia must have found out.' When Bea didn't comment, Ruth raced on, 'Well, it's obvious, isn't it? Someone his age must have been married or at least had some kind of relationship, mustn't he? I mean—'

'I haven't,' Bea broke in.

'No, but it's different for you.'

'How is it different?'

'Well, you had me and...' Ruth was suddenly floundering, and, unsure what to say, started to open the door to escape.

Bea smiled to herself and didn't try to stop her, but she couldn't help wondering what Ruth was contributing to the gossip about her own mother.

She was thoughtful as she consumed her sandwich. The gossip was probably nothing but speculation and Liam's decision to work abroad was purely a career move—or even because he had itchy feet!

That thought made Bea smile. If she hadn't met Gary, she might just have indulged her own longing to see more of the world. At the time, though, Gary, at twenty-one, had seemed so much more interesting than the boys of her own age. He'd lived in a very comfortably furnished flat and she had been impressed and flattered that he had chosen her.

It wasn't until she'd told him she was pregnant that she'd discovered he was married. His wife had been working away for a year and that had been why he'd rarely been around at weekends.

She remembered the humiliation and the despair and the hard work it had taken to regain her self-confidence. But it had been worth it, and once Ruth was settled in a career there would be plenty of time to think about visiting other countries.

She pushed her thoughts to the back of her mind and continued to see her waiting patients.

At the end of the list she was surprised to find Cilla had arrived to see her.

'What can I do for you?'

The young girl was tearful. 'I've been so sick. Almost immediately after I took the tablets this morning. The doctor said it might happen and…' Her voice trailed off and then she wailed, 'I don't know what to do.'

Neither did Bea. The morning before she would have dealt with the situation without a qualm, but after

Liam's comment about these cases the previous afternoon she would rather refer Cilla back to him for advice.

'I think you'd better see Dr Taylor again. I'll just find
out when he can slot you into his list.'

Closing the door behind her, she asked Katy who
indicated he was free at that moment.

Bea knocked on his door.

'Come!' he called imperiously.

The moment Bea set eyes on him seated behind his
consulting desk she felt the nerve endings in her skin
tingle alarmingly, giving it a warmth that she was sure
must be obvious to Liam.

She tried to tell herself it was because she was being
ridiculously over-cautious where his patient was concerned, but she knew it was more the response of her
own body to her physical awareness of him. Something
she found difficult to accept after nearly twenty years
of keeping men at arm's length because of her responsibility for Ruth.

Trying not to meet his eyes, she explained Cilla's
problem as briefly as she could. He took the notes from
her hands.

'Perhaps you'd stay nearby in case I need a chaperone. She put on a great show of modesty yesterday but
I wasn't altogether convinced. If it was that genuine I
doubt if she'd be in this predicament now.'

Bea was surprised by his vehemence. 'At least she
had the sense to come for help.'

'Hmm. I *do* wonder if she's telling the truth, though.
Was there ever a condom and is her period already
overdue? Did *you* note any sign to the contrary?'

Bea frowned. 'Of course not. I'd have told you so if
there was.'

He nodded. 'I guess so. OK. I'd better see her.'

After what he'd said about her she wondered how Cilla would feel about seeing Liam Taylor again. Had he made his disapproval clear to her the day before? It seemed not. She went readily enough.

When Cilla came out she caught sight of Bea who was hovering in her room with the door open. 'Thanks, Sister.' She was beaming. 'He's super, isn't he? I didn't know doctors could be so nice.'

Bea smiled her agreement but it changed to a frown when Cilla was out of sight. Liam Taylor could obviously charm the birds out of the branches if he set out to do so. Well, she was one who was determined not to fall.

Liam came out of his room at that moment and, catching sight of her, grinned. 'Sorry to have wasted your time. Were you just off home?'

'Not quite. I had some clearing up to do and, anyway, I'm waiting for Ruth to finish.'

'She's big enough to find her own way home, surely?'

Bea frowned. 'Of course she is, but when we're finishing at the same time it would be daft not to travel together.'

Somewhat irritated by him questioning her arrangements, and even more angry with herself at allowing a relative stranger to unsettle her, she murmured, 'That way I get help in preparing the evening meal.' Then she turned her attention to straightening the sheets on the treatment couch.

'I'm envious. I wish I had someone to share my meals.'

Feeling she couldn't do otherwise, Bea smiled wanly

and offered, 'Oh, er, can we get you something to eat later?'

'Thanks for the offer, but Alicia has suggested we eat at a new fish restaurant she wants to try. Why don't you join us?'

'Um… No, thanks. I can guess the one she means and it's not my scene. Anyway, I have to think about Ruth as well.'

Liam's penetrating blue eyes searched her face uncomfortably. 'Ruth could come, too. But tell me, why would it not be your scene?'

Really, she had never known anyone so persistent. She shrugged. 'I've outgrown places like that.'

'I think not,' he told her seriously. 'Just because you have a teenage daughter it doesn't mean you're over the age limit for fun. Or married!' He hesitated and, taking her left hand in his and examining her empty ring finger, lifted an eyebrow. 'I'm right, aren't I?'

'Maybe. Does it matter?' she queried defensively.

'Not to me,' he told her, 'but does it to you?' The look that accompanied his question was unnerving.

'No. It doesn't,' she told him brusquely. 'Now, if you'll excuse me, I must finish off here and get home.'

'If you insist.' He eyed her keenly. 'Perhaps we can continue this conversation another time.'

This was ridiculous. He was making her feel like a trapped specimen under his gaze, so as soon as she could she escaped and made her way across to the desk. Handing in the notes from her last session, she waved a hand towards Ruth and, pretending not to have a worry in the world, told her, 'See you in the car.'

'I'm going to be delayed, Mum. I'll make my own way home.'

Bea left the health centre before Liam could comment. Before the advent of Liam, her life had been jogging on smoothly. Every day had been the same and that was the way she'd liked it. She was a single mother with a full-time job that she enjoyed, and *no* complications.

As she drove home, she tried to convince herself that it didn't matter what he thought about her. His stint as a locum would be over before she knew it and her life would return to its normal routine.

Or would it? She was soon going to be home alone, something she had never experienced before. There was so much she was planning to do that she hadn't thought it would be anything of a problem. Until now, although for the life of her she didn't see why Liam's arrival on the scene should make her feel something was missing from her life!

She had worked herself up into such a state of self-righteous angst that by the time Ruth arrived home she was annoyed to discover that, because it was raining, Liam had run her home.

'I had time to kill until Alicia was ready,' he explained, 'and I thought it was an opportunity to learn where you both live.'

She couldn't quite believe what she was hearing. 'Why do you need to know?'

'You never know when your car might break down and you both need a lift to work. It can happen to any of us.'

Bea was infuriated by his calm reasoning and she refused to acknowledge it was a possibility. Instead, she said, 'I thought you said Ruth was old enough to find her own way home.'

He grinned. 'It wasn't raining then. And, anyway, I want to nip home and change out of my suit.' He checked his watch. 'I must dash. See you both tomorrow.'

'Mum!' Ruth exclaimed the moment the door closed behind him. 'What on earth made you so crabby?'

Bea ran trembling fingers through her hair. 'I really don't know. I'm sorry, Ruth. Everything seems to be getting on top of me at the moment.'

Ruth was concerned. 'Are you feeling ill?'

Bea shook her head. 'No, I'm fine.'

'Are you worried about being left alone here?'

Bea's reply was vehement. 'No way. I'm looking forward to getting on with all the things I haven't found time for over the past eighteen years.'

'You don't like Liam, do you?'

How perceptive the young could be.

'It's not that I don't like him, Ruth. It's just that he's different to the doctors I've worked with before.'

'In what way?'

'I suppose it's because he's only here for a short period and I've never had my work questioned before.'

'Questioned?'

'Forget it,' she told Ruth. 'I expect it's my hormones.'

They both laughed at the family joke. Bea's mother always blamed everything on her hormones.

'I doubt it. Most women your age are only just thinking about starting their families. You've been there, done that and once I've gone off to university you'll be free to take up new hobbies or whatever. You name it, there'll be time for it.'

Bea nodded. 'I guess so.' She'd been looking forward to it for months, until Liam Taylor had arrived on the scene. Now she wasn't so sure. He made her realise

what she might just have been missing all these years—
a male companion, a husband, a friend, a confidant.

Ruth hugged her. 'I'll be home some weekends and
it'll be the Christmas break before you realise it.'

'I know. Don't worry about it. I'm starving.'

'When Liam said he and Alicia were off to the fish
restaurant, I was green with envy. Why don't we go
there one evening?'

Bea sighed. 'I'm not sure it's the kind of place I'd
enjoy. Too noisy and too full of your kind of music.'

'You don't know until you try it. And that might be
sooner than you think. Liam seems to think it might be
a good place for a staff outing. You'd have to go, then,
wouldn't you?'

There was nothing Bea would like less, but as the
occasion would more than likely never materialise,
there wasn't much point in saying so at that moment.

Aware that there wasn't much the reception desk staff
didn't know about anyone, she asked instead, 'If Liam's
offering lifts, does he live out this way, then?'

'Yep. Apparently it's a bed and breakfast place by
the big roundabout. He says the traffic noise is horrific.
I doubt if he'll stay there for long.'

'Conveniently situated, though. I would hate to have
to exist in a B&B. Has he got furniture of his own
somewhere?'

Ruth smiled. 'Apparently not. He's planned on going
abroad for some time, so he doesn't need any. That's
something you could do when I'm at uni, isn't it?'

'What, get rid of all the furniture or travel abroad?'
Bea teased.

'No.' Ruth was scornful. 'I meant take in lodgers, but
seeing something of the world isn't a bad idea either
and you'd have your lodger to house-sit.'

Bea shook her head. Really, Ruth's imagination ran away with her at times. 'I have no intention of either taking a lodger *or* travelling. I've far too many other things I want to do.'

'That's a pity.' Ruth didn't elaborate but, knowing her daughter as well as she did, Bea was suspicious.

'Why?'

'I was thinking Liam could have my room.'

'Ruth!' Bea was scandalised. 'I don't want anyone here with me, and even if I did I wouldn't want anyone that I was working with. I don't think it would be a good idea at all. Especially a single man and woman living together.'

'Mum. It's the twenty-first century. Lots of people do it and no one thinks anything about it.'

'Well, I was brought up differently. That idea is a non-starter as far as I'm concerned, and if I ever *did* take a lodger, it would have to be a female.'

'You're an old stick-in-the-mud, Mum.'

'I prefer it that way,' she murmured as she drained the vegetables. Thank goodness she'd nipped that idea in the bud. It was bad enough having to work with Liam when he was capable of having such an effect on her. Living in the same house would be impossible.

And what about the gossip? She could just imagine it. 'Bea Seton living with a man? I'd never have expected it of her. Her daughter leaving home must have unhinged her.' Goose-bumps prickled her skin at the very thought.

'Why do you think he's still unattached then?'

'I haven't a clue, Ruth. Could be hundreds of reasons.'

After wishing Bea goodnight, Ruth slammed out of the room.

Bea didn't move but her thoughts were over-active. He'd probably had dozens of girlfriends over the years, but if he was thinking of going abroad he was reluctant to commit himself to a long-standing relationship. Perhaps, like her, the older he got the fussier he became.

Convinced now, in her own mind, that Liam Taylor was a ladies' man, she wondered why it mattered anyway. Within six months he would be gone. Determined not to admit to herself that her heart might just go with him, she slept.

It wasn't so easy the next day. Ruth was on the late shift so Bea set out in good time for work. Liam was in the waiting area when she entered the health centre and he smiled, albeit half-heartedly.

'Everything OK?' she asked.

He nodded, then said, 'If you don't mind, I'd like a word with you before your first patient arrives.'

'I'll just sort out my list and I'll be ready.'

He followed her into the treatment room and closed the door, then waited until she had completed her preparations, before speaking.

'I had a phone call from our mutual patient this morning.'

She frowned. 'You mean Cilla?'

'That's the one. She's been sick again and wants more tablets. I've asked her to bring in an early morning specimen.'

'For a pregnancy test?'

'You've got it. I'm not prepared to supply her with anything more until we're sure.'

'Right. I'll ask Katy to let me have the specimen when she comes in, and inform you of the result.'

He didn't make a move to leave.

'Was there something else?'

'Do you condone this behaviour in these young girls?'

Startled by the unexpected question, especially in view of her own past, she didn't answer immediately.

'You think it's all right, them carrying on repeatedly in this way?'

She frowned. 'Of course not. But if they sense I disapprove, they won't consult us in the future, and the result will be many more abortions. Or unwanted pregnancies. The permissive society has left us with a cleft stick.'

He nodded thoughtfully. 'So what's the answer?'

She laughed, albeit defensively. 'There isn't one. We can't change the world.' She checked her watch. 'I really must get on now. Is there anything else?'

'There is, but I didn't want to raise it in front of Ruth last night. Perhaps we could talk over a meal tonight. I mustn't delay you any longer.'

Her own behaviour uppermost in her mind as she started her morning list, Bea wondered what he could possibly want to discuss with her.

Was it work? Or the reason for his approach to it? She had to admit wondering why he appeared to be so preoccupied with the subject of promiscuity when he must have come across many more serious problems during the course of his career.

However, by the time Katy popped her head round the door to let her know Cilla had arrived, she had dismissed his interest as nothing more than an idiosyncrasy.

She welcomed Cilla with a smile. 'You've brought the specimen?'

The girl nodded and handed it over.

'If you'd like to take a seat in the waiting room, Dr Taylor will see you as soon as he has a moment.'

Bea tested the urine sample and wrote the negative result in Cilla's notes, then asked Katy to let her know before Liam's next patient was called.

It wasn't long before he was free, and she excused herself from her own patient and took Cilla's notes through to him.

'The pregnancy test was negative.'

'It *was* an early morning specimen?'

'It was certainly concentrated, but I didn't stand over her while she produced it!'

He nodded. 'Sorry. I'm not questioning your work.' She hid a smile that her sarcasm had got through to him. 'I'll see her now.'

Bea returned to her own patient, wondering what he proposed to do about Cilla, but the next man on her own list threw up a problem that drove all thoughts of the young girl from her mind.

He was a man in his early sixties who was there for a blood-pressure check. He came through when she called him.

'Hello, Mr Gray.'

He didn't appear aware of where he was and didn't answer her greeting, although he seemed to be struggling to do so. When she saw he was also finding difficulty in moving forward, she slid the treatment room chair behind him and, after guiding him into it, pressed her emergency buzzer.

Liam was the first to arrive. 'Problem?'

She nodded and, handing over the notes with a frown, said, 'A stroke, I think. He's one of Alicia's patients.'

Liam was joined by John, the senior partner, and,

after asking Bea what had happened, between them they carried out a thorough examination on the man.

'Hello, Mr Gray—Jim. Remember me? Dr Adams? And this is Dr Taylor. We just want to take a look at you.'

Throughout their checks they spoke his name repeatedly but with minimal response, so it wasn't long before the two doctors nodded their tacit agreement.

'We need to get him to hospital,' Liam told Bea. 'I'll try and organise an ambulance quickly so that we can free your room.' He left, taking the notes with him.

John returned to his own consulting room to continue seeing his patients, and Bea was left alone with Mr Gray. She held his unaffected hand and talked to him, and she was pleased to note an occasional flicker of interest in his eyes.

Liam was back very quickly. 'All arranged. I've scribbled this note to go with him. Everything OK?'

She nodded as Liam joined her beside Mr Gray and spoke to him slowly, explaining what was going to happen. He seemed to understand and Liam went on to reassure him, 'We'll let your wife know where you are.'

The ambulance men arrived at that moment and they all assisted in moving the ill man onto the stretcher. As Bea released her hand, it came into contact with Liam's. Startled by the arousing effect of the contact, she snatched it away.

Momentarily meeting his eyes, she was sure he'd experienced something similar, but he quickly averted his gaze and she couldn't be sure.

When Mr Gray was safely on his way to hospital, Liam thanked her for her prompt action and all she'd done since. 'I must ring his wife now and let her know what's happened. Then I'll get back to Cilla. I know you must have a huge backlog by now, but if you've a moment at lunchtime, I'll update you on what's happening.'

He was right about the backlog. It was nearly one before Bea had finished seeing all the people waiting for her. Clutching her usual sandwich, she made her way to the coffee-room on auto pilot.

Liam looked up as she entered and sprang up to switch the kettle on. 'Sit down. You look all in.'

She nodded. 'A coffee will revive me.'

He handed her a steaming mug and she asked, 'Did you speak to Mr Gray's wife?'

He frowned. 'Not yet. I haven't been able to contact her.'

'How did you get on with Cilla?'

She wasn't sure she really wanted to return him to the subject of promiscuous females, but she thought she ought to ask.

'I talked to her for a long time this morning and I think I'm beginning to understand where she's coming from.'

'Coming from?'

'She's looking for love and approval. Something she's never known in her short life. It didn't need to be sexual love, but the boyfriend was the one to turn up.'

'How long has she known him?'

'A week.'

'So it's unlikely she was pregnant before this episode?'

'Very. I now understand her fear of me examining her. She's only slept with him once and didn't think much of it. Then this happened and he told her she must see a doctor. Frightened her to death, so she's been drinking heavily to try and forget about it.'

'What on earth has she been drinking?'

'Rough cider.'

Bea raised her eyebrows in horror. 'No wonder she's been sick!'

'Exactly. I think we got a few things sorted out this morning.'

'I'm pleased to hear it.'

Bea was pleased in more ways than one. Cilla had obviously emanated vibes that had intuitively worried Liam, and that was why it seemed as if he disapproved, giving Bea the wrong message altogether.

'What time would you like to eat tonight?'

'Oh, er, I'm not sure...'

'I've a couple of patients to see later this afternoon so I'd prefer it not to be too early. Would seven be OK?' He clearly wasn't giving her a chance to change her mind.

'Seven would be fine.'

He grinned. 'I'm looking forward to it. Anywhere special you'd like to eat?'

As she believed his invitation was merely to talk about work, she didn't think it important. She shook her head.

'I want it to be somewhere you'll really enjoy.' He looked at her questioningly.

'You choose.'

'Right. Only the best is good enough for you, so I'll ask John which restaurant he recommends.'

As he went in search of John, she couldn't help smiling. He certainly knew how to make a woman feel good. If she wasn't careful, she'd find herself not only physically attracted to him but liking him just that bit too much.

CHAPTER THREE

'BEA.'

She was still so immersed in her thoughts about Liam that she jumped and turned at the sound of her name to find the senior partner looking at her with concern. She had prepared her room for the afternoon clinic and, having heard nothing more from Liam about Mr Gray, was on her way to his consulting room to ask.

'Is something the matter?'

'No, er, no. I was miles away.' She guessed the heat she felt rising in her cheeks belied her words, and tried to cover her confusion by adding, 'It's been a busy morning. I was just wondering how Mr Gray was faring at the hospital.'

'I rang a few moments ago. There's not a lot of change. He's undergoing a barrage of tests. Does his wife know what's happened?'

She shook her head. 'Liam said he couldn't contact her and that he would try again later, but I haven't heard if he succeeded.'

John Adams smiled warmly. 'Liam was a good choice, wasn't he? Hopefully Barry will be back in harness before he disappears off to Malaysia.'

The thought of Liam leaving caused Bea's stomach to flip uncomfortably. She tried to pull herself together and asked about their colleague. 'Have you seen Barry this week?'

John nodded. 'Last night. Two weeks away from this place and he looks the picture of health, but I've told him to take his time. The pain was clearly a warning, and as we now have Liam on a six-month contract there's no point in Barry rushing back.'

'You think he *will* be back?' Bea had never voiced her doubts before, but Barry was in his late fifties and had suffered a couple of severe angina attacks.

'Difficult to say, Bea. But we must keep the option open for him.'

'Too true. And as you say, Liam is ideal as he wants to move on in six months.'

'You don't sound exactly thrilled by that thought.'

Bea shrugged noncommittally.

'Too many changes at once, perhaps? Or is it just that you're worried about Ruth leaving?'

She laughed. 'You've got it in one. It's the first time I've realised Ruth has grown up and I can't help wondering how she's going to cope.'

'Don't you worry about Ruth. It's you we ought to be worrying about,' John told her.

'Me?' Bea gave a nervous laugh. Surely the effect Liam was capable of having on her wasn't *that* obvious.

'Yes. You're going to be on your own for the first time in eighteen years. How are you feeling about that?'

'Great!' Relief that that was all he meant caused her to release the breath she hadn't realised she'd been holding. 'I can't see there'll be any problem, John. I've got my work and the vacations will soon come round and, anyway, I'm planning to do so many things I've never found time for in the past.'

He eyed her doubtfully. 'Ruth was saying she thought it might be an opportunity for you to travel. Isn't it something you've always wanted to do?'

'Ruth! I don't believe it. If she thinks I'll be able to

afford holidays abroad, as well as supporting her through her degree, she can think again.'

'You could work abroad. Like Liam's doing.'

An irrational fear washed over her. What was John suggesting? That she appeared so attracted to the new locum that she might follow him to Malaysia?

The sooner she put a stop to any such idea the better. 'I've no intention of making a move anywhere while Ruth is a student. I would hate to be on the other side of the world if she needed me.'

John shook his head, but before he could respond Ruth arrived to start her late shift. She joined them in the waiting room and looked expectantly from one to the other. 'Why so serious? Was—is it a patient?'

Bea laughed as John replied, 'Heavens, no, child. We wouldn't discuss patients out here. We were talking about you.'

She pouted. 'That makes you glum? Why?'

'We were discussing the financial implications of a university education,' John told her with a grin. 'In other words, how much you're going to cost your mother over the next few years.'

Ruth demurred. 'I won't cost her anything. I'll work through all my vacations and get a student loan.'

Liam, who'd emerged from his room a moment earlier, must have overheard what was being said and joined them.

'If I were a betting man, I'd place a huge stake that you'll not only cost her money but peace of mind as well.'

'Huh! Things have changed. Students are self-sufficient these days.'

Liam appeared amused by Ruth's spirited defence.

'*Some* students always have been. I had no parents to bail me out.'

Bea and John turned to look at him, their eyes asking the same question.

He grinned and told them hurriedly, 'OK. So perhaps I was exaggerating.'

Bea sensed they had just heard something of profound importance about Liam, something he didn't share very often and something he was already trying to pretend was insignificant. She searched for the right way to respond.

John did it for her. 'That must have made your decision to work abroad easier.'

Liam shrugged uncomfortably. 'Not really. I probably feel I owe more to the people who took me on. But you were talking about Ruth, not me.' He flashed her a wicked grin. 'Is there something I should know about our young receptionist?'

John took the hint that he wanted to change the subject, and with one eyebrow raised he teased, 'Well, now. Where shall we start? I think it'll have to be when Bea joined the team here because that's when I first met this energetic bundle of trouble.'

Ruth opened her mouth to protest at the description, but her mother was too quick for her. 'Least said soonest mended, especially as the afternoon patients are arriving.'

Ruth took her place in Reception and Liam followed Bea into the treatment room.

'I gather we work together on this list.'

Bea nodded. 'But you only need to be on hand if there's a problem. I can easily deal with the straight-forward smears.'

'Fine. I'll wait in my room, then.' He riffled through the notes. 'Any problems you know of already?'

'Jane Finn, third on the list, I think. She had treatment at the hospital after an abnormal smear, and the colposcopy was followed up by two smears at the hospital. This is her first one back here. I've been warned she's very uptight and doesn't really believe she has nothing to worry about.'

'Would you like me to have a chat with her?'

'It could be useful. The appointments are booked at twenty-minute intervals and I hate to run late. So many of the women are nervous about the test.'

'I'll do that, then. If she arrives early I'll talk to her before you see her, otherwise I'll make it afterwards.' He was thoughtful for a moment. 'Wouldn't they prefer a female doctor on standby?'

Bea grinned. 'They would, but Alicia refuses to be pigeon-holed to deal with women's problems and, anyway, she's on that course today. She doesn't mind doing some weeks, but not every week. That's why I trained to do the smears.'

He nodded, but as he returned to his room he was obviously deep in thought, and Bea wondered if it was because he wanted the best for his patients and felt Alicia was being unreasonable.

Pleased that perhaps everything about Alicia didn't meet with his approval, Bea started her list with a feeling of contentment she hadn't experienced since Liam's arrival on the scene.

Apart from Jane, Bea only had to ask Liam to see one other couple that afternoon. But he didn't have it easy. The two consultations took up most of his time. Jane needed a lot of reassurance. Bea did her best while she was actually taking the smear sample, then suggested that if Jane was still worried she have a chat with Liam.

'It took me almost an hour to convince her she wouldn't be dead and buried within the year,' Liam told Bea over a cup of tea when she'd finished her list. 'And the rest of my afternoon was spent trying to sort out the Crays.'

Bea nodded. 'I can't imagine why they didn't ask to see someone before this, especially when there's so much in the women's magazines about infertility and the ticking of the biological clock.'

'There's nowt so queer as folks, me dear, as I've learnt to my cost.' He chuckled and reverted to his own voice. 'I do wonder if, when she first stopped the Pill, she was half-hearted about having a child. I think her career was still very important to her at that time. The pressure has probably only been on since she was made redundant last year. And I got the feeling that he came with her today because, even now, he's keener than she is.'

'Could be a problem, especially as they've left it a bit late. Haven't they?'

He shrugged. 'Maybe and maybe not. We won't know until we get the result of the various tests we'll be doing. I've taken a detailed medical history from them both and we'll go from there.'

'Now, time to forget the Crays and go in search of Mrs Gray. Do you want to come with me, or shall I pick you up later to eat?'

'I'll come with you, if that's OK. I'll leave my car keys with Ruth. She can use it to get home tonight.' Having done so, and cautioned her daughter to drive carefully, she told him, 'Perhaps I can be of some help. She's bound to be upset.'

Liam smiled warmly, apparently pleased by her decision. 'Patients aren't just a nine-to-five chore for you, are they?'

Bea frowned as he led the way to his car. 'I don't think of patients as a chore at all. I enjoy my work. Mostly, anyway.'

'I phrased that rather badly, didn't I?' He helped her into the passenger seat of his car. 'I was trying to let you know how impressed I am by your dedication.'

Bea laughed and when he slid into the driver's seat beside her she said, 'Now you're going over the top the other way. I like to get satisfaction from my work and I wouldn't if I left on the dot every day.'

Liam grinned. '*Touché.* I'll settle for that.' He swung the car into a steep close. 'I think it's number fifteen we're looking for.'

She checked the notes on the dashboard. 'Yep. And that's it over there. The green door.'

'Unlucky colour,' he muttered.

'Unlucky?' she queried.

'My old granny would never have green paintwork or furnishings in the house. Said it would bring bad luck to the occupants.'

'And you believe it?'

He laughed. 'It's been ingrained in me from childhood. I'm sure there's no truth in it, but I still wouldn't risk painting my own walls green.'

He climbed from the car. 'Wait there a moment while I see if she's in.'

The door was answered at his first ring and Bea climbed from the car and joined him as he introduced himself.

'It's Jim, isn't it?' Mrs Gray was already anticipating the worst.

'He's in hospital, but doing OK,' Liam reassured her quickly. 'We've been trying to contact you all day.'

'I've been in London. You'd better come in.'

She led the way into a sitting room that lacked any homely touches of clutter.

'What happened?'

'Your husband came for his blood-pressure check and suffered a slight stroke while he was with us.'

As her left hand lifted to her mouth in horror, Liam took the other one. 'If he was going to have one, it was the best place to do it. We had him in hospital in no time.'

Noting Mrs Gray's frozen expression, Bea asked, 'Can I make you a cup of tea?'

Mrs Gray shook her head. 'I have one poured.' She shuddered. 'I nursed his father with the same. For eighteen years. He died two years ago.' Tears began to trickle down her cheek. 'I'm just beginning to get my life back together again.'

Liam's glance towards Bea spoke volumes. This was something they didn't know and were going to have to deal with.

Bea brought the mug of tea through from the kitchen and handed it to Mrs Gray. Her heart went out to the woman. She must have been tied to the house all that time and she was obviously terrified of losing her freedom all over again. 'Your husband was already responding when he left us.'

Liam joined in her reassurance. 'There's every chance he'll make a good recovery, especially with all the facilities available these days. It's very different from twenty years ago. I'd take a bet that they didn't have a stroke rehabilitation unit in his father's day.'

Mrs Gray shook her head, but Bea could see she

didn't believe Liam. All she could see ahead was another twenty years of being tied to an invalid.

'Look, why don't we take you to the hospital now, and you can see him for yourself and speak to the hospital doctors who'll be taking care of him?'

She nodded wanly. 'I'll do that, but I can drive myself. Thanks for the offer, though.'

They stayed while she drank her rapidly cooling cup of tea and Liam told her which ward her husband was on. 'Isn't there someone who can go with you? Have you family nearby?'

She shook her head as she rose to her feet. 'I'll be all right. There's just the two of us. Thank you for letting me know. You've enough to do without that.'

As she showed them to the door, Bea said, 'Contact me at the health centre if there's anything at all I can do, even if it's only for a chat.'

Mrs Gray nodded hopelessly and closed the door behind them.

'Poor woman,' Liam ground out furiously as they made their way back to the car. 'Why do some people get all the bad luck?'

'I don't know, but they do. And it's so unfair. All you can say is that they're usually the people strong enough to cope with it.'

He swung round to look at her. 'Do you really believe that?'

When she didn't answer, he muttered, 'I'm afraid I don't. I've seen too many go under with the weight of their problems.'

Bea didn't know how to respond. She had an uncomfortable feeling he was talking personally, rather than about his patients.

In the end, she waited until they were back in the car

and said, 'Whichever, there's not a lot we can do about it, is there?'

He shook his head. 'Sorry about that outburst. I just felt so helpless in the face of that woman's misery.'

'All we can do is pray that he'll make a good recovery, and give her as much support as she needs. I'll contact her first thing tomorrow.'

'You'd better liaise with Alicia if they're her patients.' Bea nodded as he continued, 'Right. Work forgotten. John's told me about a couple of good restaurants.' He named them. 'Tell me which you prefer.'

Bea had to admit she didn't know. 'I've heard about them, of course, but haven't tried either. I'm happy to get us something if you don't mind the wait.'

'I promised you a treat and a treat it shall be. We'll try the Italian place near the town bridge.'

Treat? Why did he see the need to provide a treat? Had she just given him the idea that she never went out?

The sooner she remedied that the better. 'I've had so many late nights recently, it might be better if you just took me home.'

'Why on earth should I do that? Surely I'm allowed to spoil you for once.'

Bea groaned. 'What have you heard about me? That I'm a stay-at-home recluse that needs to be winkled out of her shell?' If that was what was being said, she'd better let him know about some of the different activities she was involved in.

He turned to her and laughed. 'You don't believe I'd listen to health centre gossip, let alone believe it?'

'No more than I do,' she told him heatedly.

'So you've heard the rumours circulating about me?'

'Well,' she murmured defensively, 'Ruth has tried to involve me, but…'

'You couldn't refuse to listen,' he teased.

'It's difficult. I've always taught her that gossip can be destructive…'

Liam smiled wryly. 'But now she's beyond your control?'

'I—I suppose so.'

'She's a very competent young lady. You did your job well.' He chuckled. 'Almost too well.'

'Wh-what do you mean?'

'Well, she certainly has her fair share of confidence.'

'Is that a criticism?' Bea felt colour sear her cheeks and knew she didn't want it to be, especially having agreed to go for this meal with him.

But did it matter? Her need to deny herself because of her responsibility for Ruth was over. Perhaps, perhaps…this was an opportunity to dip her toes in the water of a relationship without too much commitment on either side. And she had to admit she was sharply aware of a dangerous sense of excitement every time he was near.

'Come to a decision yet?' he enquired with an enigmatic smile.

'Decision?' She hesitated. 'Y-you mean about the Italian restaurant?'

'No. I mean about me!'

The colour burned in her cheeks even more fiercely. 'What decision do I have to make about you?'

He shrugged. 'You were so deep in thought I guessed you were weighing up my good and bad points. I wondered which had come out on top.'

She gave a nervous laugh. 'I wasn't thinking about you.'

'No? Who, then?'

'I, er, I was really thinking about what you'd just said about Ruth. It's not easy for parents to get the balance right.'

'Balance?' He thought for a moment.

'I was determined she wasn't going to turn out a shrinking violet. As far as I can see, the up-and-coming generation won't get very far in this world without confidence.'

He laughed. 'As long as it's only the up-and-coming generation, we don't have to worry about it.'

Miffed by what she saw as his mockery, she subsided into her seat and refused to look at him when he rested a hand over hers.

'I'm saying all the wrong things, aren't I?' he told her gently. 'I think you've made a marvellous job of bringing up your daughter and that you're doing a wonderful job at the health centre. There, am I forgiven?'

Sure he was now just sweet-talking her, Bea didn't answer. He parked the car and helped her out, kissing her lightly on the lips as he did so.

'The world will look a better place after we've eaten.'

Her reaction to the brief touch of his lips was so intense that she barely heard his whispered words. His kiss had aroused sensations within her that she couldn't even recall experiencing on that fateful night with Gary.

Fearful that Liam might notice her bemusement, she turned and strode ahead of him in the direction of the bridge. He followed and said, 'Hey, wait for me. I'm hungry, too.'

His words nearly stopped her in her tracks, and she told herself to lighten up. He was talking about food—plain and simple! The Italian meal he had suggested.

She forced herself to turn and look at him and speak normally. 'It's a long time since either of us have eaten.'

She was relieved to see he appeared oblivious of her confusion and pushed open the door.

A rotund, moustachio'd Italian man bustled forward and at Liam's request showed them to a table for two. With a flourish, he provided them each with a menu the size of an opera score!

The moment they were alone Liam said quietly, 'I can hardly believe such a typical Italian restaurant owner exists.'

She grinned. 'He is rather over the top, isn't he?'

He turned to the wine list at the back of the menu. 'Wine?'

At her nod he asked, 'White or red?'

She shrugged. 'Whatever goes with the seafood cannelloni.'

He nodded and flipped to the main menu. 'That sounds good. I'll join you. Anything to start?'

'The Italian salad with the blue cheese dressing, I think.'

He gave their order, including a minestrone soup for himself. 'And a bottle of number eleven, please.'

'I've ordered a Chardonnay—Australian. Hope you'll like it.'

'I'm sure I will.' She hadn't a clue about wines, but on the few occasions she'd tried them she'd enjoyed most of them.

The bottle arrived cradled in a bucket of ice. The waiter poured a drop for Liam to try, then filled both their glasses.

Liam raised his glass and said again, 'I hope you like it.'

She took a sip. 'It's lovely. Very refreshing.'

He watched her obvious enjoyment and smiled. 'You're relaxing. Good. Now perhaps I can chat to you without you taking things the wrong way.'

She immediately tensed. 'Chat? About what?'

'About you taking a lodger.'

'A lodger?' she echoed. 'I don't think so. I'm looking forward to having my own space for the first time in my life.'

'That's a pity, because John thought it would be a solution to both our problems if you could see your way to letting me stay for the short time I'm in Bargate.'

'John!' Bea exploded. 'I don't believe it. Does no one in that place mind their own business? Or are Ruth and John colluding to run—or ruin—my life?'

'I didn't realise Ruth had already made the same suggestion—but I'm not surprised. You probably don't realise it but I quickly recognised what a tight-knit group you all are at the health centre. Almost an extended family, with John as the father figure.'

Bea sighed and counted to ten. 'Perhaps, but—'

He didn't let her finish. 'You're a popular member of the team. They all care about what you're going to do when Ruth finally takes off.'

Embarrassed now, Bea was at a loss as how to answer.

When she didn't speak immediately, he probed gently. 'Perhaps it's a proposal you aren't prepared to entertain?'

'You mean taking a lodger? No...er...it isn't only that. It's...'

'Yes?' he prompted hopefully as she searched for the right words.

'Well...' She shrugged. 'I suppose I don't imagine

you would enjoy someone from the health centre keeping tabs on your private life.'

As his eyebrows shot up into his hairline, she knew she'd said the wrong thing and tried to make a joke of it by saying with a half-laugh, 'I know I wouldn't want all I do revealed to—'

But he was so taken aback by her suggestion that he didn't appear to hear and broke in on her explanation. 'What on earth do you think I'll be doing when I'm not at work? Slave-trading, pimping or perhaps you see me as a drug-pusher?'

The waiter arrived with their starters at that moment and Bea struggled hard not to laugh at the waiter's wide-eyed horror.

'Enjoy your meal,' he told them hurriedly, before scurrying away to the kitchen.

When his gaze locked with Bea's, Liam could maintain his indignation no longer, and they both spluttered with stifled laughter.

'He heard what I was saying, didn't he?' Liam asked.

Bea nodded. 'I'm afraid so. At this moment he's probably urging the owner to call the police!'

The meal was superb and as it came to an end Bea realised that Liam had the knack of getting her to talk about herself while telling her just enough about himself to lull her into believing she was listening rather than talking. But she noticed that he carefully didn't make any reference to his parents or family and wondered why.

Over coffee, he returned to the subject of moving into her home.

'I don't want to put you under any pressure—' his tone was gently reassuring '—so if you have a good

reason for refusing, I'll forget the idea here and now.
But if not, it seems it could be a mutually convenient
solution.'

Having just allowed herself to relax and enjoy his
company, Bea groaned inwardly. 'I suppose so.'

He must have heard the doubt in her voice. 'So, what
do you say to a trial run?'

'Ruth doesn't move out yet and—'

'If you have room it might be easier for us all if I
move in before she does.'

Startled, Bea knew her cheeks were tinged with colour as she queried, 'Easier? In what way?'

He laughed. 'It's been my experience that people who
live alone get set in their ways and resent them being
disrupted. I've been there and it's not an easy situation
to handle. And if you're worried about trusting me, I
can provide plenty of references.'

She laughed dismissively. 'That's not a problem.'
She hesitated, before saying, 'I'll give the idea serious
thought but I need to discuss it with my daughter first.
Especially if you're going to move in before she leaves.'

'I'm not hassling you. I need to give notice where I
am.' He leaned across the table and rested a hand over
hers. 'If you do agree, I promise to be a good tenant
and behave myself. You won't regret it.'

She pretended indignation. 'I should certainly hope
not.'

He asked for the bill, preparatory to leaving. 'OK?'

Bea nodded, but as they walked to the car she wondered if it really was. Was she being railroaded into a
decision she wasn't sure about? And was she far too
aware of this man to ever feel comfortable living under
the same roof?

As if to answer her question, he slid an arm around

her shoulders, and his touch provoked an involuntary response from her body.

She pulled away abruptly.

'Hey, what are you afraid of?'

'I'm not.'

'Strange. I would say that was a clear indication of fear.'

'Not fear,' she protested. 'Common sense. If we're going to even consider this idea we should start as we mean to go on!'

He turned her towards him so he could see her face.

'And what way is that, may I ask?'

CHAPTER FOUR

BEA ignored Liam's query and said instead, 'It's time I was home. Early duty in the morning.'

He sighed with exasperation at her evasiveness and briefly she thought he'd actually detected the emotions she was trying so hard to conceal.

Telling herself she was perfectly capable of handling this situation, even if she hadn't had much experience of men, she pulled her jacket round her to cover the hardening of her nipples which would surely make the response of her body obvious. And despite the emotional storm he was capable of arousing within her, she had no intention of making the same mistake twice. Especially with someone who was only a transient member of staff.

When he pulled up at her front door, she thanked him for a very enjoyable evening and asked, against her better judgement, 'Would you like to round it off with a cup of coffee?'

'I think not tonight, thanks. As you said, it's late and we both have to be up early in the morning.' He searched her face closely. 'I do appreciate the offer, though. I believe it could mean you're starting to trust me.'

For the third time that evening Bea cursed the ready tendency to blush that accompanied her red hair.

'I said I didn't want references, didn't I?'

'So you did.' He grasped her arms gently and pulled her towards him, dropping a light kiss onto her lips as he had done earlier. 'Goodnight, fair Beatrice. And thank you.'

She drew away from what she considered a perfunctory gesture. As she watched him drive away, she was mortified that she had believed, even for one moment, that his invitation that evening could have been for any other reason than to discuss the letting of her empty room in a congenial situation.

Her thoughts were a jumbled mass of questions. Why was he so keen to move in? Was he just looking for a more comfortable pad? Or was he so tuned into the health centre grapevine that he felt sorry for her being left alone when Ruth left? If so, he needed to be disabused of the idea, otherwise working with him for the next few months would be impossible.

To Bea's great relief, Thursday morning didn't give her much time for thought, but by lunchtime she was exhausted. The girls on Reception pushed so many extra patients into her list that she didn't stop for a moment, so when the last person left she was in desperate need of a cup of coffee.

Leaving her desk cluttered with the morning's paperwork, she slipped across to the coffee-room and switched on the kettle. She was so deep in her thoughts of what she still had to do that she jumped when Liam said behind her, 'Is there enough water to make one for me?'

He placed his hands on her arms and said, 'Here, steady on. I didn't mean to frighten you.'

She turned to face him. 'I didn't hear you coming.'

He searched her face with a frown. 'Problems?'

'No—none,' she responded hastily, then, realising

he'd been referring to the patients, she added, 'Not unless you count overwork, that is.'

'Overwork?' he echoed solemnly, his eyes teasing. 'That sounds ominous.'

'It was one of those mornings when everybody needed to be seen, whether they had an appointment or not. I've still got a mound of paperwork to bring up to date.'

'Anything I can do to help?'

She shook her head. 'I needed this reviver first, that's all.'

'Do you have a clinic this afternoon?'

'Diabetic. Today's list looks quite reasonable, thank goodness.'

He shook his head. 'It seems as if there's more than enough work for one person. Has John thought about employing another nurse?'

'The idea's been mooted, but…' She shrugged.

'Not financially viable?'

'I can't quite see how it would work.'

'The post wouldn't need to be full time.'

'I was thinking more about the rooms.'

'I'm sure something could be arranged.'

She nodded. 'In the meantime, my paperwork awaits.' She returned to her room and closed the door. As a locum, Liam probably had time to waste, but she didn't, especially if she wanted anything of a lunch break. She checked her watch. Twelve-fifteen already. He was right, she did need help. She was always too busy to even think about it!

When Ruth arrived to start her late shift, she came in search of Bea. 'I brought you a sandwich. You were so late up I knew you couldn't have had time this morning.'

Bea jumped up and hugged her. 'You don't know how good that sounds. I was just wondering if I could find time to nip out and buy one. I haven't stopped all morning.'

'I heard you about in the night. Is everything OK?'

Bea nodded. 'I just didn't sleep very well.'

'Didn't you enjoy your dinner with Liam, then?'

'Of course I did. But he left me with a lot to think about.'

'Like what?' Ruth probed eagerly.

'John seems to have had the same idea as you. He suggested the possibility of Liam moving into your room when you go to university. As I said to you, I don't think it would be a good idea.'

'Why not? Are you afraid of what he and Alicia might use it for?' Ruth teased.

Bea looked up. 'Ruth!'

'Lighten up, Mum. You'd only be renting a room, not inviting him to share your bed!'

'Ruth, you're becoming incorrigible. This isn't something I want to rush into, but Liam suggested he might move into the spare room while you're still around. But neither do I want to dismiss it out of hand. So during the night I was trying to work out the details we'd need to settle if I agreed to the idea.'

'What details are needed?'

'Financial. And there's only the one kitchen, isn't there?'

'Um. I didn't think that would be a problem.'

Bea shook her head with a fond smile. 'You didn't think, full stop!'

'I just thought you'd go on the way we do. Whoever's home first cooks the meal.'

'Sometimes!' Bea teased.

'I do it most times. I reckon you're trying to find a way out. What are you frightened of?'

'I'm not frightened. But I will be if I don't get on with this, and Katy's probably looking for you to relieve her.'

'In other words, get lost.' Ruth flung out of the room with a grin.

Bea thought fondly about her daughter while eating her sandwich.

Her diabetic clinic wasn't taxing and Bea was able to leave on time, so she decided to visit the supermarket.

She was trying to recall what their store cupboard needed, which prompted the thought that it would need to be much more comprehensive if Liam did move in, when her trolley clashed with another.

She looked up to see the devil she was thinking of grinning behind the offending cart. 'I was only preventing you crashing into that display of baked beans. You didn't appear to have noticed it.'

'What—? Oh...' She felt the usual colour flaring in her cheeks as she saw how near she had come to making a spectacle of herself. 'Thanks. I would have felt a fool if that lot had toppled down on me.' She was about to move on when she frowned. 'I thought you were doing evening surgery.'

He nodded. 'I am.' He glanced at his watch. 'I'm just grabbing something to eat afterwards.'

She glanced into his trolley and saw a couple of oven-ready meals nestling between packets of crisps and chocolate bars. 'You're not into healthy eating, then?' she teased.

'What's wrong with vegetable lasagne?'

'Nothing. It's the crisps and chocolate bars I'm worried about.'

'Perhaps they're not for me,' he taunted.

Bea wasn't about to let him get away with that. 'So, you're leading someone else into bad habits?'

'Now, would I do that?' He checked his watch again. 'Much as I'd love to continue this conversation, I must dash. Perhaps we can take it up another time?'

'Ruth's covering the evening surgeries so we'll be eating late this evening. You're welcome to join us for something a little more substantial.' She felt so sorry for anyone who had to dine alone on food that wasn't freshly prepared that she made the offer without first debating whether it was a good idea.

He accepted immediately. 'Sounds wonderful. I'll bring Ruth home with me. OK?'

As she watched him replace the ready meals back in the cabinet and grab the crisps and chocolate from the trolley to pay for at the basket-only checkout, she groaned inwardly, wondering why she had been so impetuous!

She couldn't retract the invitation now, so all she could do was search out the ingredients she would need for a meal for three. She settled on chicken served in a red wine sauce.

It was far from ready when she heard his car pull into the drive.

'Hi, Mum, we're here and we're starving.' They made such a noise coming through the front door that her call was unnecessary.

'I'm in the kitchen.'

Ruth banged back the door as they joined her. She put an arm around her mother and peered at the casserole being seasoned. 'That smells good.'

'I'm glad about that but it won't be ready for another hour.' She turned to Liam. 'Meanwhile, would you like a coffee or something stronger?'

'A coffee would be great. Anything I can do to help?'

Bea shook her head. 'All under control. All it needs is time. Perhaps Ruth would show you her room. If it's presentable. Otherwise you could see what you think of the spare room.'

'That's always ready for use,' Ruth said with a laugh. 'In case one of us is ill, or we have an unexpected visitor, or the roof blows off, exposing us to the prying neighbours!'

Hearing Liam chuckle as Ruth led the way into the spare room, Bea felt hot colour stain her cheeks as she realised she had just given implicit agreement to him moving in. Something she certainly hadn't intended without knowing him better.

She was thoughtful as she replaced the casserole in the oven and rinsed her hands. He was so easygoing and amiable that it was difficult to understand why a man of his age with a high earning potential was prepared to put up with renting rooms only suitable for students. There was certainly something mysterious about him, and yet she had reread his CV and there seemed to be nothing untoward in that to give her a clue.

Had he been married, or cohabited with someone, and it had gone wrong? Perhaps, as the gossips suggested, a woman had taken him to the cleaners and he couldn't afford much rent. Despite his complete authority at work, there was an air of vulnerability about him that had made her catch her breath on more than one occasion. And invite him for this meal!

When they came back downstairs, she said, 'Could you set the table, Ruth, and I'll get Liam an aperitif?'

'What about my aperitif?'

'I'll find you a can of Coke. What can I get you, Liam?'

He was studying her so intently that she was impatient for his answer so that she could escape his penetrating gaze.

After a few moments thought he replied, 'I'd like Coke as well, if it's not too much trouble.'

Bea made her way into the kitchen and retrieved three cans from the refrigerator. 'Come through to the sitting room, Liam.'

She indicated a seat, but before he sat down he closed the door of the room and again searched her face intently. Bea turned away to find some glasses.

She handed him his Coke and, after thanking her, he said, 'I thought you were beginning to trust me, but I was wrong, wasn't I? You're still not happy about this idea.'

'Why do you say that?'

'You're on edge as if you regret inviting me this evening.'

She opened her mouth to refute his accusation, but he prevented her response by adding, 'Why don't you trust me?'

When she didn't speak, he said in a soft voice that couldn't be overheard, 'Perhaps you're right not to.'

His smile as he finished speaking was disarming and infuriatingly it made her heart race uncomfortably.

'Why…why do you say that?'

He shrugged. 'If you'll never relax with me in the house, perhaps we should just forget the whole idea.' He leaned forward and took one of her hands between

his, before telling her gently, 'My confidence has re-
bounded from all the knocks it's had. I get the impression that yours still needs a bit of bounce put back in
it.'

'Well, thank you for trying, Liam Taylor. What do
you suggest? An infusion of dog food?'

She had been about to add that they'd only known
one another for a few days when his low, rumbling
chuckle stopped her. His gently caressing thumb was
playing such havoc with her thought processes that, instead, she was tempted to blurt out that her agitation
was solely because she felt so attracted to him.

Horrified that she was even considering such an admission, she released her hand and lifted her glass.
'Cheers.'

Before he could respond, Ruth bounded into the
room. 'The timer's pinging. Can we eat now?'

Bea gave Liam a rueful smile. 'No concessions for
age in this house.' She led the way into the kitchen.
'All right if I serve onto the plates in here tonight?' she
asked as she lifted warmed plates from the oven.

'Fine by me.' Liam took the oven gloves from her
and lifted out the casserole.

When their plates were filled, they carried them
through to the dining room.

'We *usually* eat in the kitchen,' Ruth told him with
the candour of a teenager.

'Saves a lot of work,' he observed mildly, with a
lopsided grin in Bea's direction.

The chatter over their meal was dominated by Ruth,
and Bea was glad of the opportunity it gave her to think.

'That was fantastic,' Liam told her after he had consumed every morsel on his plate. 'If I do move in here
I can see I need to brush up my culinary skills.'

Bea shrugged. 'I don't mind if you prefer to live on ready meals.'

He regarded her with surprise. 'You think we should eat separately?'

'Well, I hadn't really thought about it. I thought you would prefer that. I, er…'

'You don't intend to wait on me hand and foot, is that it?' He grinned. 'I can assure you I wouldn't expect that for one moment. I'm perfectly capable of taking care of myself.'

Her colour flaring, Bea protested. 'I—I— As I said, I hadn't really thought about it.'

'But, Mum,' Ruth broke in, 'we talked about it earlier. Don't you remember? I said I imagined whoever was first home would cook the meal.'

Bea groaned inwardly as she regretted instilling the need for honesty into Ruth. 'I, er, I suppose you did say something of the sort, but I didn't give it much thought as I had patients waiting.'

Liam picked up his plate and carried it to the sink. When he turned on the tap, Bea followed him and rested a hand on his arm. 'There's no need for that, Liam. Taking in a lodger is a new experience for me and I'm not sure what's expected of me, or if I should lay down house rules before you move in.'

He turned off the stream of water and turned to face her. 'I haven't thought of myself as a lodger. I thought as we are friends and business colleagues we could proceed on an informal basis, but if you'd rather formalise the proceedings, I'll buy a rent book tomorrow and we'll do just that.'

Aware how deeply she had offended him, and how it was the last thing she'd wanted to do, she asked, 'Coffee?'

The look Liam directed towards Ruth, who was standing behind them, precipitated her into action.

'I'll make the coffee, Mum. You two go and sit down and thrash out the ground rules for living together.'

Bea gasped at her daughter's unfortunate turn of phrase—or had it been deliberate? Then she led the way into the sitting room, unable to meet Liam's gaze. When he took the seat opposite her and she finally did so, she discovered he was having difficulty in keeping a straight face.

Her own laughter bubbled up and spilled out then, and when she could eventually control it she said, 'You can always trust Ruth to call a spade a spade!'

He was still chuckling as he murmured, 'Perhaps we should formalise the agreement after all. I certainly don't want to tarnish your reputation and standing at the health centre.'

She said quietly, 'As an unmarried mother, I guess it's a little too late for that.'

He leaned forward and, taking both her hands in his, murmured, 'It seems to me that you have an unnecessary hang-up about something that happened so many years ago.'

She swallowed hard, trying to ignore his touch. 'Not really. I've had to live with my mistake for nearly twenty years but I've never regretted Ruth's birth for one moment, rather the contrary.'

'But you feel you ought to have provided the regulation two-parent home for her to grow up in?'

'Maybe I did once but, quite honestly, she's a much more balanced personality than many of her friends who *have* had two parents.'

'It must have helped, having your parents as role models.'

She remained silent, unwilling to confide the reaction of her parents to her pregnancy which at the time had left her in no doubt of her wickedness.

'Can someone open this door for me?' Ruth shouted.

Liam leapt to his feet and did so, then took the laden tray from her and placed it on the coffee-table.

'Well, have you sorted it?' Ruth asked.

Before Liam could speak, Bea told her, 'We'll share the kitchen duties, like you said.'

Liam looked up at her with a surprised grin. 'I promise I'll do my fair share. And pay my way.'

Conversation over their coffee was again dominated by Ruth, which gave Bea time to mull over what he'd been saying.

Did he have hang-ups as well? He'd mentioned the lack of parents to support him through university, but everything else he'd told her had been about his life since qualifying.

She longed to find out more, but, although the time would have been right a few moments before, to do so now in front of Ruth would be a mistake. She would have to wait for another opportunity.

When he had finished his coffee, he asked, 'Can I wash up?'

Bea shook her head and replied, 'No duties tonight. You haven't moved in yet!

'If you're sure, I'll leave you to it. Thank you for the delicious casserole, Bea. I'll see you both tomorrow.'

Bea remained where she was, strangely sad that she had at last met a man who could stir her heart but who would soon be moving on.

Friday morning's surgery was busier than ever. It was nearly one by the time Bea's last patient left and she was gasping for a cup of coffee. She dashed across to the staffroom and switched the kettle on, absently spooning coffee into her mug as she mentally agreed with Liam that it really was time she had the help of another nurse.

She had just returned to the treatment room with her coffee when there was a knock on her door and Liam poked his head round. 'Have you a minute, Bea?'

She nodded and he came in and closed the door. 'Katy's just had a call from the radiotherapy centre to say that one of our patients didn't show up for treatment yesterday and isn't answering her phone.'

'Who's that?' Bea thought she probably already knew.

He consulted the paper in his hand. 'Sharon Gimby. I'm the only doctor in at the moment so I've read through her notes, but Katy tells me you spend a fair amount of time with her.'

Bea nodded. 'She hasn't had an easy life and—'

'She's had a bloody awful life according to these.'

'I know.' Bea sighed. 'Do you want me to go and see if she's at home?'

'How are you fixed time-wise? I thought I'd do a home visit, but as you know her it might help if you were there as well.'

Bea nodded and checked her watch. 'I can spare three quarters of an hour, but I must be back by two-thirty. I've several repeat dressings coming in then. Just let me finish this coffee.'

Liam's answering smile was sympathetic. 'I hate to ask you when you so obviously need your lunch-break, but I would be grateful.'

'Give me five minutes.'

When she'd finished updating all the records on her

desk, she grabbed her jacket and went in search of him. 'Ready when you are.'

As they made their way out to the car, he said, 'I spoke to John last night about getting you some help. He seemed quite agreeable. I think he's too close to the problem to have realised just how busy you are.'

An appreciative warmth spread through her at him caring enough to first recognise the need and then to tackle John on her behalf. 'You're probably right. I've just accepted it was the norm. It sometimes takes a new-comer to see what's needed. I'm very grateful.'

'I also suggested we should perhaps have practice meetings or at least a meal together so that things like this can be discussed.'

'Ruth did say you'd thought about the new fish res-taurant for that!'

'I mooted the idea, but John turned it down. Alicia, too. I don't think she enjoyed our outing there.'

Because of the food or the company? Bea wondered. She certainly hadn't seen much of them together since that evening. 'Perhaps it would be best to let John pick the venue.'

'I think you might be right.' Liam's words were ac-companied by a smile that did amazing things to her pulse rate. She strove to ignore it, and instead concen-trated on the reason for their visit.

'Sharon hates anyone she doesn't know to see her face. If you don't object, I'll explain who you are first.'

'Fine.'

'Horrific as her notes are, they don't really tell the whole story.' It took the remainder of the journey to give him the details.

When he pulled the car to a halt in front of Sharon's terraced house, she climbed out and rang the doorbell.

The curtains were open but there was no reply. Bea shrugged towards Liam and, having peered through the window and seen nothing, she shook her head and rang the bell again.

No response.

She tried the houses on either side, but there was no answer from either.

She returned to the car. 'She has a home care assistant one day a week, and I'm pretty sure she'll have a key. Perhaps we could contact Social Services and try to find her.'

Liam spent the next half-hour on his mobile phone, trying to contact someone who wasn't at lunch, but he had no success.

'I'd better take you back for your dressing appointments and keep trying.'

'As soon as I finish I'll go out there and try again. In the meantime, I'll check if she's turned up for her radiotherapy today.'

'I'll do that.'

Between each of her afternoon patients Bea's thoughts turned repeatedly to Sharon. What on earth could have happened to her? She was so anxious about her health that Bea couldn't believe she would miss even one appointment without good reason.

Mr Darby was her last patient of the afternoon, and she was thrilled to see how well his burnt skin was healing.

Liam must have noticed him arrive, and she had just removed the old dressing when he knocked on the door and asked, 'Do you mind if I come in and see how it's progressing?'

Mr Darby smiled and said, 'Come in, Doctor. It's going on a treat.'

Liam examined the area. Straightening up, he said, 'That's incredible. I expected it would take much longer to heal. I must use that regime again when I'm dealing with burns.'

Bea nodded and waited for Liam to leave before re-dressing the area. She had a problem. She'd forgotten to tell Liam that she hadn't been able to use the dressing he'd ordered, and she couldn't do so in front of the patient and undermine his confidence in the locum. But he was so impressed by the result of the dressing he thought he'd ordered that she knew she would have to confess the truth.

When Mr Darby left, she cleared the treatment room and went in search of him.

'Ah, Bea. Just the person. Sharon missed her appointment today as well. I've located the address of the care assistant, but she's not in at the moment. I've spoken to the local police and they say it's OK for us to go in if we have the key-holder with us.'

'They prefer not to become involved?'

'I suppose you could say that.'

Bea handed him Mr Darby's notes. 'I have a confession to make.'

'Yes?' His query was accompanied by one corner of his mouth lifting in amusement. 'What's that?'

'I didn't have the dressing you suggested in stock, so I used Flamazine, which in any case I thought prefer-able. I don't want you to go away with the wrong idea…well, about the efficacy of the dressing you or-dered.'

'I *was* surprised when you didn't tell me what you had used this afternoon.' He was grinning like a Cheshire cat.

'You knew!' she accused indignantly. 'Did you expect me to tell you in front of Mr Darby so that he would think I know more than you?'

Still smiling, he shook his head. 'I wondered how he was getting on so I checked his notes yesterday. I was very impressed by your initiative. The last place I was at had very limited stocks, which is why I prescribed what I did.'

To her horror she felt herself blushing fiercely. 'It wasn't initiative. It was a case of using what was available. And when I saw how well it was working, I continued with it.'

'Please, don't feel you have to make excuses. I consider doctors and nurses should work as a team and, I can assure you, I'm always open to suggestions.'

It was Bea's turn to grin. 'I'll remember that! Now, let me have Mrs Bell's number and I'll try and contact her.'

'I'll do it.' He rang immediately and raised his eyebrows to indicate his success.

When he replaced the receiver, he told her, 'Mrs Bell will meet us there in a quarter of an hour. She said Sharon seemed in good spirits on Wednesday, so she doesn't understand what can have happened.'

This time Liam didn't stay in the car, but after they had rung the bell he took the key from Mrs Bell and opened the door, then allowed the two women to precede him inside.

Bea repeatedly called Sharon's name, but there was no answer. 'It's Sister Seton, Sharon. From the health centre.'

There was still no reply so Mrs Bell led the way upstairs.

Everything was neat and tidy and the home care assistant gasped. 'She hasn't slept there since I changed the bed on Wednesday.' She turned back the top. 'See, it's all clean, and, anyway, if she'd been here the room would be a tip by now.'

They all trailed back down the stairs and were discussing what to do next when Liam thought he heard a noise in the kitchen. He looked out through the back window into an enclosed yard.

'Can't see anything and the door's locked.'

'Any details in her notes about a next of kin?' he asked.

'I don't think there is one. That's part of her trouble. She—'

Bea broke off as she, too, heard a muffled sound. 'Is this a cupboard?' she asked Mrs Bell, pointing to a latched door under the stairs.

'It's the cellar. Never used these days.'

Liam opened the door and peered down into the blackness. 'I've a torch in my bag.'

Bea handed it to him as the noise they had both heard became more audible.

'I'm going down,' he told them. 'Stay there.'

They did as they were told and then they heard him give a gasp of horror, but when Bea asked what he'd found, he didn't immediately reply.

'What is it, Liam?' she asked again.

Bea was relieved to hear what sounded like Sharon's voice repeating something over and over again, but Bea couldn't make out what it was.

Guessing she was probably terrified of an unknown man approaching her, Bea called down, 'Hi, Sharon. It's Sister Seton. From the health centre. Remember? Dr Taylor, who's down there with you, is a locum doctor.'

She heard a muffled oath, then Liam shouted, 'Call an ambulance, Bea. Sharon's at the bottom of the steps. She must have fallen.'

CHAPTER FIVE

BEA snatched up his mobile and dialled. After giving the address, she told Mrs Bell to watch out for the ambulance and then called to Liam, 'I'm coming down.'

'Can you find something to make her more comfortable first? And be careful. These steps are lethal.'

She ran upstairs and pulled a pillow and blanket from the bed. When she started the journey down, she could hear him reassuring Sharon that he really was a doctor and that Mrs Bell had let them in. 'Sister Seton will soon be down here to help us both,' she heard him say gently.

He shone the torch onto the tortuous steps to guide her feet, and spoke again to Sharon. 'You've obviously done some mischief to that right leg, but hopefully that's all. We'll soon have you out of here and tucked up in a warm bed.' He called up to Bea. 'When you get down here, I can take a better look.'

She was just five steps from the bottom when she stupidly lifted her head to take a look at the scene below her. The next moment she felt herself skidding on her back down the remaining steps.

Liam caught her as she struggled to stop herself falling onto Sharon.

'All right?' he asked anxiously, before attempting to release her.

Trying to find a replacement for the breath she had knocked out of herself, Bea could only gasp, 'I will be.'

He gently massaged her back, his touch causing such

a delicious fluttering up and down her spine that she knew she must stop him before she became even more breathless.

'Sorry about that,' she murmured. 'I'm OK now. Let's take a look at Sharon.'

'If you're sure.' He pulled into a gentle hug, before reluctantly releasing her.

They made their patient as comfortable as they could on the hard and filthy floor, then Bea held the torch while Liam examined Sharon for any further injuries. 'Thank goodness, the leg seems to be the only problem.'

Sharon squinted up at Bea with narrowed eyes, then launched into a long-drawn-out wail that for a moment drowned the siren of the approaching ambulance.

Bea crouched beside her and smoothed her brow gently, before taking hold of her hand. 'Try not to make too much noise, Sharon, or we'll never hear the ambulance men.' Her voice was soothing and the wail stopped instantly.

'There's rats. I seen them moving.' Sharon's voice was rising again and it took all Bea's self-control not to scream herself when something ran over her foot.

'Do you need a stretcher?' With relief, she recognised a paramedic at the top of the stairs.

'I don't think so,' Liam called, 'but she needs her leg splinted before she's moved.'

'Right. Back in a jiff. Fred's just gone for the lamp.'

Fred was soon down with them, his lamp illuminating the cellar so that he and Liam could check Sharon's condition more thoroughly.

'How long've you been here, love?' Fred asked her.

She shook her head. 'A week, I think.'

Liam shook his head and said quietly, 'More like a couple of days.'

After immobilising the injured leg with an inflatable splint, the paramedics made short work of getting her up the stairs and into the ambulance, but throughout the rescue Sharon was uncooperative unless it was Bea who asked her to do something.

Eventually, Liam and Bea followed them out. 'Can we leave you to lock up the house, Mrs Bell?'

'I'll see to that.' She set off upstairs to check that all was secure.

Liam turned to Bea and rested a hand gently on her shoulder. 'Is your back OK?'

'Fine—just a little bruised.'

He hugged her gently again and said, 'You did well down there. I wonder, Bea, as she's responding to you and only you, do you mind going in the ambulance with her? I'll pick you up from the hospital—providing I can still drive after the vicious kicks she gave me with her good leg before you joined us!'

Bea couldn't prevent a wicked grin stealing across her face. 'She did mention seeing rats, I believe!'

'I'll remember that.'

It was only a short journey and Liam was there by the time Sharon was wheeled into Accident and Emergency.

'I'll stay with her,' Bea whispered to Liam. 'I'll get a cab back to collect my car.'

'You'll do no such thing.' He looked her up and down with a smile. 'Have you seen the state you're in? I doubt if any respectable cabbie would let you near his vehicle.'

She looked down at herself and then at Liam. For the first time since they'd climbed up from the cellar Bea realised just how grimy they both were, but *she* looked as if she'd been rolling around the floor.

'How come you kept so relatively clean?' she demanded.

He grinned wickedly. 'Because I had a handmaiden to do the dirty work for me.'

She gave him a threatening look. 'My turn to get even with you!'

'Promises!' he teased. 'I'll come and relieve you after evening surgery's finished or, if you're ready before that, give me a ring there and I'll sort you out a lift.'

It was nearly an hour before Sharon was seen by an overworked casualty officer, who immediately sent her for an X-ray of the injured leg and alerted the orthopaedic team that she would need admission as the fractured bone had broken through the skin.

During the long wait, once she had been given something to help the pain, Sharon dozed fitfully.

Bea took the opportunity to go to the washroom and get off the worst of the grime.

When Sharon was awake, Bea chatted to her, eventually asking her, 'What were you doing in the cellar? Mrs Bell said it's never used these days.'

Sharon sniffled, 'I thought—I wanted to find a book I used to have when I was a little girl. I'd looked everywhere. Then I remembered, when I was small, Mum kept odd bits and pieces of mine down there. I thought it might be among them.'

'Did you find the book?'

'I never looked. I dropped the torch and it went out. I climbed back up the steps but the door wouldn't open. It swung to behind me, but I didn't realise the latch had dropped. I didn't know what to do so I came down the steps again to try and find the torch, but I fell.' Huge tears trickled down her cheek as she recalled her fright.

To try and take Sharon's mind off the fall, Bea asked, 'What was the book?'

'It was all about a family in America. Two boys whose baby brother had died and their uncle came to look after them. I read it over and over because it finished happily and made me feel so warm. They were so sure their brother was in heaven that they talked to him. I wanted to read it again.'

Bea thought hard for a few moments. 'I think I once read a book like that. Was it called *Helen's Babies*?'

'That's it. That's the name,' Sharon said excitedly. 'Have you got a copy?'

'I don't think so.' Bea shook her head, aware that she had thought it extremely dated when her mother had suggested she read it. From the clear disappointment on Sharon's face, it was obvious she needed it, probably as an emotional security blanket, and Bea resolved to search out a copy.

'I'll ask my mother if she still has it.'

Sharon closed her eyes happily at the thought. At that moment the porters came to take her to the ward via the operating theatre, and Bea decided it was a good moment to leave.

She checked her watch and, guessing Liam must have finished his evening surgery, walked to the main entrance to see if she could see any sign of his car. It was parked right opposite the doors, but there was no sign of Liam.

She paced up and down irritably. Where on earth was he? She felt like a freak and just wanted to get home and into a bath.

'Hi. How's Sharon?' She swung round and saw Liam and Ruth approaching.

'Just gone to Theatre. Where *have* you been?'

'Looking for you.' Liam frowned at her curt response. 'Are they going to pin the bone?'

She nodded.

'How was she in herself?'

'As well as can be expected.'

'I ran so late I kept expecting you to ring.'

'The A and E department is stretched to the limit. I wouldn't have been surprised if Sharon had had to spend the night on a trolley. Can we get away from here and chat later?'

She knew her tetchiness was unreasonable and he must be as tired as she was, but she couldn't help herself. She turned to Ruth as Liam helped her into the front seat. 'Why didn't you bring our car and save Liam the double journey?'

Ruth looked at her with surprise. 'I couldn't, Mum. You had the keys.'

'Of course. Sorry.'

'It's been a long day for you, Bea. I thought we'd eat out. You look all in.'

'Thanks for the compliment,' she muttered as he started the engine.

She knew she ought to be grateful but she was exhausted physically and emotionally and she just wanted to get home. 'I can't go out looking like this.'

'Ruth and I discussed it. We called at the house and she's brought you some clothes. You can wash and change at the surgery.'

'Is that all right, Mum? We thought we'd go to the bistro just round the corner in Church Street, rather than me getting a meal at home. Liam didn't think you ought to drive.'

Realising they'd only been thinking of her, Bea nodded her agreement before resting her head on the head-rest.

When they arrived at the health centre, Liam turned to her. 'Give Ruth your keys. She can take your car and grab us a table. I'll wait for you. I want to collect some notes while I'm here.'

She did as he'd suggested and took the clean clothes Ruth handed over. But as she started towards the building she stumbled on legs that suddenly seemed too frail to support her.

He took the bag of clothes and grasped her around the waist, murmuring contritely, 'I dragged you away from your lunch and I bet you haven't made up for it since.'

Sure it was nothing more than his nearness that was causing the problem, Bea shook her head as she tried to move away, then wished she hadn't. He pulled her closer to him, and when the earth stopped spinning she tried to smile reassuringly. 'I often miss lunch.'

'But you don't usually work twelve hours on an empty stomach.'

He was right. She hadn't even had a drink since that rushed coffee at the end of her morning list. She could have got one from the machine in the hospital, and had nearly done so, but it wouldn't have been fair to drink it in front of Sharon, who hadn't been able to eat or drink because she would be having an anaesthetic.

For some unfathomable reason Bea wanted to burst into tears. It had been a pig of a day and Liam was being just too considerate.

She saw Ruth watching her with concern so, swallowing hard, she struggled to pull herself together.

'Is something wrong, Mum?'

Liam said briskly, 'Nothing that a good meal won't

put right, so the sooner you get over there and organise things, the better.' Ruth didn't need telling twice.

He unlocked the surgery doors and released Bea so that he could switch off the alarm.

He dropped the bag of clothes onto a waiting-room chair, and as she was about to lift it he stayed her arm with his hand, pulling her towards him to kiss her gently.

'I've been waiting to do that since I saw you waiting so forlornly in front of the hospital door.'

It was too much for Bea. The tears of exhaustion which had been threatening flowed unchecked, and as he pulled her closer and gently massaged her back, they soaked into the shoulder of his jacket.

The storm within her eventually abated, and she pulled away, saying, 'I must change. Ruth will wonder where we are.'

'Let her...'

He tried to move her nearer again, but she let out a gasp of horror. 'Liam. Your jacket. It's streaked with dirt.'

He looked down at his shoulder and grinned. 'Worth the cleaning bill.'

'The sooner I get rid of all this dirt, the better.'

Despite his attempt to detain her again, she made her way to the staff washrooms and, after washing off all the dust and grime that was left, slipped over her head the dress he had brought for her.

She wished it had been anything but the lowest-cut number in her wardrobe, an emerald green, plunge-neck jersey knit that left little of her cleavage to the imagi-nation, and also revealed every contour of her body.

What on earth had possessed Ruth to decide that was a suitable outfit? She could guess. Ruth thought all her clothes were fuddy-duddy and had persuaded her to buy this dress for a backstage party they had both been invited to the previous Christmas, together with the other members of their theatre club.

She had felt uncomfortable wearing it then, and felt even more so now, but Ruth, no doubt, thought it was the only fashionable item in her wardrobe.

Angrily, she brushed her hair with fierce strokes and deliberately omitted applying any make-up.

Liam was seated in the waiting room when she emerged and he gave a low whistle. 'Some transformation. You should wear that colour more often.'

Noting his gaze lingering on the revealing neckline, she muttered, 'This is once too often for this dress. I should have sent it to the charity shop long ago.'

'It's beautiful, Bea, and so are you.' He rose from his seat as if in a daze, but when he tried to encircle her with his arms Bea backed hurriedly away towards the door and said airily, 'Time to eat, I think.'

He sighed and locked up behind her.

Once they were settled in the car, he rested a hand on her knee. 'I'm sorry if we did the wrong thing, Bea, but Ruth said that once you got home you'd refuse to come out again and then you'd insist on helping with the meal and the clearing away.'

Annoyed with herself that she had made him feel he had to explain, she felt the colour flaring in her cheeks and murmured ruefully, 'I expect she was right.'

Obviously relieved, he turned and grinned at her before bringing the car to a halt in the bistro car park.

They made their way to the table where Ruth was anxiously waiting. 'I wondered where you'd got to. Are you sure you're all right, Mum?'

Bea smiled warmly. 'I'm fine, love. It was good of

you and Liam to do all this.' But even as she said the words she began to worry that Ruth might be seeing Liam as the father figure she had never had. In which case it would be better if Liam didn't move in until Ruth had left for university.

Deciding she couldn't begin to think about such important matters, she buried her nose in the menu.

Liam asked if they would both like the dish of the day. It was *Navarin d'agneau.* 'In other words, lamb stew,' Liam said with a laugh.

They both concurred, and he asked if it could be served as soon as possible and also ordered wine and mineral water.

'Nothing alcoholic for me,' Bea told him. 'Not when I have to drive.'

'You don't. Ruth'll drive your car home.'

The lamb was delicious and Bea indulged herself with a dessert for once. When she'd finished eating, she felt much better. She had been careful not to touch her glass of wine until she had well lined her stomach, and by the time they left she felt almost human again and able to cope with anything.

Apart from Liam telling Ruth that if she took the car he'd bring her mother on later.

'That's silly, Liam. It's out of your way.'

'Maybe. But I want to talk to you.'

Bea frowned. 'About work?'

'Partly.' He didn't elaborate until Ruth had driven off, then he turned to her and said, 'She's a big girl now.'

'Sorry, Liam. But it's been one hell of a day. If we have to discuss this, at least we could find a more suitable time!'

'I quite agree.' He took her in his arms and touched

her lips with his, not the light caress of earlier but a deep and probing kiss that was way beyond the boundaries she usually set in her relationships. Especially as one of his hands had already searched out the inviting neckline of her dress.

But, then, no one before had ever made her feel the way Liam did. How was she going to protect herself from such a destructive attraction? He only had to look at her in a certain way to make her toes curl. She shuddered as she recalled the storm his touch had aroused within her earlier.

She raised her outstretched arms and pushed him gently away.

'I need to sleep, Liam,' she told him quietly.

As he drove her home, she fell into a deep sleep. He watched her tenderly, aware that it had been her air of trusting vulnerability which had attracted him that first day, and as he'd got to know her better he'd become incensed that she had to work so hard and he'd tried to make life easier for her.

Her utter exhaustion that evening had made him realise that she needed someone to care for her sooner rather than later. But he shouldn't have rushed it. He still had over five months to get to know her better and, providing he was given a clean bill of health, to persuade her that he had at last met the one person he believed could make him happy.

What a bind that he'd already committed himself to a twelve-month contract in Malaysia, his health permitting. It had seemed like a good idea when he'd discovered there was little chance of a recurrence from his testicular cancer. Sure it would be better for his foster-parents if he was out of the country, he'd intended to move abroad earlier, but the scare over his health had prevented it.

Perhaps all wasn't lost. If his final check-up with the oncologist was clear, he would feel he had a future to offer Bea. With Ruth away at university, perhaps she would agree to go out there with him. Hadn't both John and Ruth told him that Bea had always wanted to travel, something she hadn't managed to do while she'd had a child at home?

Bea woke the moment the car came to a standstill outside her house and, after thanking Liam for the meal, leapt quickly from the car. He watched her indoors, wondering when *would* be the right time for Bea.

Ruth was already in her room and Bea went straight to bed, but despite her exhaustion she tossed from side to side, aware that she had one big problem. She was falling in love. It was as simple as that. But this time it was with a man who wouldn't be in the same country for that much longer.

Working with him without letting him know wasn't going to be easy, and living under the same roof with him would be well nigh impossible.

So the sooner she withdrew her offer of a room the better. She could probably just about last six months of encountering him at work, but sharing a home with him was out of the question. She'd been mad to agree to it, because there was no doubt in her mind. She wanted Liam and she wanted him in a way she didn't even remember happening with Gary.

Her feelings for Liam were a whole new experience, but she couldn't handle giving herself to someone she felt this way about, only to watch him walk out of her life within a few months. And that was what would happen. Without a doubt.

She eventually gave up all hope of sleep, and got up to make herself a cup of tea. As soon as she thought it a reasonable hour, she rang the hospital to discover how Sharon was getting on. She was put through to the orthopaedic ward.

'Staff Nurse Deacon speaking. How can I help you?'

'Hello. I'm the practice nurse at the Bargate Health Centre. I brought Sharon Gimby in last night—she's one of our patients. How is she?'

'Well, the operation went well, but she's very tearful this morning. She's lying with her face to the wall and refuses to move or talk to anyone.'

'Hmm. I'm not surprised. She hates anyone to see her face.'

'It's not as bad as some I've seen,' the staff nurse rejoined quietly.

'I know, but she has so many other problems her self-esteem has reached rock bottom.'

'She has no next of kin?'

'Nobody, and I suppose I'm the nearest to a friend she has. She comes in and talks to me sometimes.'

'Will you be visiting her?'

'Yes, when I finish work.'

'Could you bring in her toilet articles and night-clothes?'

Bea was silent for a few moments. 'Could be difficult. Her care assistant tells me she has neither.'

'I see.'

'I'll try and get to the chemist's before I come this afternoon.'

'We'd better ask the hospital social worker if she can find her some nightwear. We'll see you later, then.'

Bea was thoughtful as she made her way in for the

Saturday morning surgery, especially when she discovered that Liam was standing in for John.

Before he had a chance to speak to her she called her first patient, and as he worked through his own list their paths didn't cross. The moment eleven o'clock came, and there was no one waiting to see her, she escaped.

'I've got a lot to do, Katy, but I can be reached at home if necessary.'

'Shouldn't need to disturb you. The test match has just resumed on TV. It's quite a nail-biter.'

Bea bought a pretty toilet bag for Sharon and filled it with the necessities for a hospital stay, then made her way home. Ruth had obviously just rolled from her bed and was sitting by the telephone, yawning widely.

'That was Liam. For you.'

'Damn. Does he want me to ring him back?'

Ruth shook her head. 'I told him to come round.'

'Not again! He's been at the health centre for less than a week and is already nearly living here. Strikes me he needs to be allowed to get himself a life of his own.'

Ruth was startled by her outburst. 'I thought you'd changed your mind about him.'

'Changed my mind? In what way?'

'You didn't like him much at first, did you?'

'I've never disliked him—'

'Well, I think he's good fun. And I said I'll take him shopping this afternoon. Do you want to come?'

Bea shook her head. 'I've promised to visit the woman I took into hospital yesterday.'

'On a Saturday!'

'She has nobody else.'

'I can think of much better things to do.' Ruth

screwed up her nose in disgust and went upstairs to shower.

Bea primed the coffee-maker and started the washing machine she had loaded earlier.

When the doorbell rang Ruth hadn't reappeared, so with a sigh she answered it.

'Problem?' she asked shortly as Liam followed her in.

He frowned. 'Didn't Ruth say what I wanted?'

'She's in the shower. Your call must have woken her.'

'I rang the hospital when I'd finished my list. I gather you're going in to see Sharon this afternoon.'

She nodded.

'Why?'

'What do you mean, why?' Bea asked irritably. 'She'll talk to me and she needs to talk.'

'And?'

'I don't know what else you want me to say.'

'I hate to see you working such long hours that you're too tired to enjoy life.'

'Yesterday was a one-off.'

'So what interests do you have outside work?'

'What interests? Well, I go to aerobics with Ruth and we go to the theatre sometimes. And I'm involved with the local church—'

'I asked what interests *you* have. Interests that will continue once Ruth has left home.'

'All of them, and I have my work and my professional meetings. I won't have time for a lot more.'

'Don't try and tell me your workload at home will be increased, because we both know it won't. Without Ruth to look after, life will be much easier, especially as I don't believe she does as much around the house as you so fondly make out.'

'What are you trying to say, Liam? And why?'

'You might be the mother of an eighteen-year-old, but you're only thirty-six. You should be living life to the full.'

Wasn't she? Over the years she'd thought that she'd had the best of both worlds. She'd enjoyed her work and she'd been out with the occasional man, but for Ruth's sake she'd finished any relationship when it had started to get serious.

'Shouldn't you?' he prompted with a frown.

Realising he expected an answer, she tried to recall what the question had been. But for the life of her she couldn't. Apart from the fact that it had made her angry.

'Shouldn't I what?'

He attempted valiantly to hide his exasperation, but Bea could read it plainly in his eyes. 'Be enjoying life to the full.'

'Oh! But I am. And Ruth has brought me more happiness than I would ever have thought possible and I…I have plenty of friends…and—'

'And you have no idea what you're missing.' He cut short her attempt to convince him, but before he could elaborate Ruth joined them, her hair backcombed into an outrageous frizz.

'Are you staying to lunch, Liam? I missed breakfast, so I'm starving.'

'When are you not?' He laughed.

Ashamed of her lukewarm welcome, Bea rushed in with an offer she hadn't intended to make. 'You're welcome to eat with us, but it'll only be a sandwich.'

'If you stay, Liam, we can hit the shops that much earlier,' Ruth cajoled.

'I'll stay if you make the sandwiches, Ruth.'

'But...' Bea was about to argue, but the look Liam directed her way silenced her.

'OK.' Ruth trotted off happily to the kitchen.

'Let her do it, Bea. *You've* done a morning's work already.'

Unaccustomed to anyone considering her needs, she did so, but the feeling of warmth he'd engendered was tempered by what was surely a veiled criticism of her not making Ruth do her fair share of the household chores.

She resorted to sarcasm to defend herself. 'Don't forget I'm only thirty-six. I can still just about manage to do my job and look after myself and Ruth.'

'But you shouldn't have to.'

'Most working wives and mothers do it.'

'Perhaps, but most of them have a man in their life to share the load,' he told her softly.

She laughed. 'I'm not sure I believe that. A man would probably make more work, not less.'

He searched her face intently, before saying quietly, 'Is that why you've never allowed another man into your life?'

She was stung by his suggestion and retorted, 'I've been out with men in the past, but I haven't wanted, or needed, any of them to share my life.'

'They fell short of your ideals? Your memories of Ruth's father?'

Furious, she sprang to her feet, but before she could protest Ruth burst through the door with a tray containing a mound of sandwiches and three mugs of coffee. She stopped abruptly, looking from one to the other. 'Oh...er, am I interrupting?'

Bea strove to control her voice. 'Nothing of importance.'

Liam didn't speak but the look he gave her sent her stomach into a spin before he turned and took the tray from Ruth and placed it on the coffee-table.

They all sat down and Ruth tried valiantly to keep the conversation flowing, but neither of them responded above words of one syllable.

The moment Ruth had cleared away the plates and mugs, Liam rose. 'We'd better get out of your hair now, and let you get off to the hospital.'

His tone told her nothing, and as the things she wanted to say couldn't be said in front of Ruth, they would have to wait.

'Thanks for lunch,' he told her as they left. 'Perhaps I could take you both for a meal this evening?'

Start how you mean to go on, Bea told herself. 'I'm afraid *I* can't. I've made other arrangements.'

She knew Ruth was looking at her with surprise and willed her to keep quiet, though she supposed there was little hope of that once they were alone.

'Perhaps I can take Ruth to TGI Friday's then. I'm sure it wouldn't be your scene.'

The door banged behind them and Bea groaned despairingly.

What was the matter with her? Why couldn't she accept that Liam would be on the scene for just six months and enjoy the time, being cosseted for once. For he really did seem to have her welfare at heart.

Surely it would be a bonus for her to enjoy his friendship for that short time, especially as he might just be right about how she would feel when Ruth left home.

As she hung out the washing and got ready to visit

Sharon, she went over their conversation in minute detail.

If only he knew! Gary was the last man she would consider as the ideal mate. True, she'd thought she'd loved him at the time, but she'd soon recognised it had been nothing but a rebellion against her strict upbringing. She was no longer sure *how* she'd felt about him.

It certainly hadn't been love. With hindsight she doubted if it had even been a schoolgirl crush.

She thought about Liam and knew with a sudden clarity that the way she felt about him was very different. He was a man worthy of her love, which Gary had never been. But he would never know how she felt. She would see to that.

Her eyes wet with unshed tears, she moved restlessly about the room, straightening the cushions, tweaking the curtains into place. Then she snatched up her jacket and set off to visit Sharon.

As she got out of her car, she saw Mrs Gray doing the same in the next bay. She smiled and asked, 'How's your husband?'

'The doctors seem very pleased with his progress. Perhaps, like your doctor said, they can get him self-sufficient before he comes home. They do seem to be doing a lot for him.'

Bea smiled. 'For your sake, I hope so. But don't forget to contact us if you have a problem or just need to talk.'

Mrs Gray nodded. 'I'll tell Jim what you said. I know he's been as worried as me, but things don't look quite so hopeless today.'

The nurse in charge of the ward that afternoon was concerned about Sharon. As she'd been told, Bea found her lying with her face to the wall. 'Hi, Sharon. It's me—Nurse Seton from the health centre. How are you feeling today?'

Sharon turned slightly towards Bea and then, catching sight of her interested neighbours, looked away again.

Bea drew the curtain slightly to shield her from prying eyes and said briskly, 'No one can see you now. Come on, sit up for a few minutes.'

Sharon did as she said, and Bea handed over the toilet articles she'd bought. 'How about brushing your hair for a start?'

Slowly, Sharon did as she suggested.

'Have you washed today?'

'The nurse did it.'

Bea nodded her approval. 'And how about dinner? Did you eat some?'

'A little.' Bea already knew that wasn't true.

'You're going to have to do better than that if your bones are going to heal.'

Sharon nodded dully. 'I don't really care.'

'Well, I do. I'll miss you popping into the health centre for our little chats.'

Sharon looked at her with surprise. 'Really?'

'I wouldn't say it if I didn't mean it.' She watched Sharon's expression change to wonderment as she realised there really was someone who cared.

'If I go and see if I can find you something to eat, will you at least try?' The staff nurse had told her there was a salad for Sharon in the kitchen, so Bea made her way there. When she returned she said to Sharon, 'The potatoes were past their best, so I binned them, but I found a roll and butter instead.'

She handed the tray with the plate of ham salad over,

and Sharon made short work of it. 'There's some fruit and custard. I'll go and find it.'

That dish was cleared as well. The nurse assigned to Sharon was amazed. 'That's much better. And there'll be a cup of tea soon.'

Having noticed the facial scars on the lady in the next bed, Bea persuaded Sharon to let her draw back the shielding curtain and speak to her. 'This is Sharon Gimby. She's feeling much better since she had something to eat.'

'I'm Freda. What are you in for?'

Bea watched Sharon, hesitantly at first, then with increasing confidence, converse with Freda. Bea listened to Sharon tell of her fall and then mention her previous accident.

When the tea arrived, Bea said she must be going.

Freda nodded. 'We'll be all right, won't we, Sharon? Sounds like we have lots in common.'

Bea walked away from the ward with a sigh of relief. She'd guessed by the scarring that was visible on Freda that she'd probably been in a car accident and would have some residual degree of disfigurement.

What she'd hoped for when she'd introduced them seemed to be working. If only Freda stayed on the ward long enough to get Sharon over her fear of facing strangers and to realise she wasn't the only one with a problem, this accident could have a happy outcome and Sharon could relegate her past to where it belonged. To the past.

Bea left the hospital and climbed into her car and asked herself why she herself hadn't done just that. The more she thought about it, the clearer it came to her that she was just as guilty as Sharon of trying to hide from her past—something that wouldn't have occurred to her but for Liam's outburst that morning.

Perhaps she did need to start to live again. With that in mind, she went to the most outrageously expensive boutique on the outskirts of the town and bought herself a silk dress and jacket which she had no idea when or where she would wear, and then took herself home for her quiet evening in front of the television, only stopping off to buy herself a ready meal!

CHAPTER SIX

'YOU'RE back early.'

'So are you.' Ruth retorted. 'Where did you go?'

Bea smiled and tapped her nose, then, turning to Liam who had followed Ruth in, asked, 'Coffee?'

At his nod, Ruth hastened out to the kitchen, much to Bea's surprise.

They sat in silence for what seemed an eternity and then Liam asked, 'How was Sharon?'

He'd thrown her a lifeline and she seized it eagerly. 'Much better by the time I left. Not only was she refusing to talk, but she wouldn't eat either. Luckily they'd kept her lunch back. I persuaded her to eat most of it. Then I introduced her to the lady in the next bed, who had some facial scarring, probably following a car accident.

'When I left Sharon was telling her her life history. I couldn't believe it. She's always been so withdrawn. Perhaps this accident will have done Sharon a good turn. I do hope so—'

'Whoa, Bea.' With a smile, Liam raised a hand to stop her in mid-flow as Ruth returned with the coffee. 'You don't have to say another word to convince me your visit was worthwhile. I'm very impressed.'

Feeling foolish, she said curtly, 'You did ask!'

He leaned forward and took her hand, saying softly, 'I know I did and I'm really pleased to hear your visit was so successful. I know I would find visiting someone like Sharon a nightmare.'

'I don't see why. *You* get on well with everybody.'

Ruth handed them their coffee.

'How was your meal?'

Ruth wrinkled her nose. 'All right, I suppose. We couldn't get into Friday's so I suggested that new place in the square. Not to be recommended.'

Liam laughed. 'You wouldn't recommend anywhere that didn't have junk food on the menu. You just don't appreciate good home cooking.'

'She eats it here!'

'That's the problem.' Liam grinned.

'Are you suggesting—?'

Liam broke in on Bea's indignation to placate her. 'Don't take it personally. She's got to rebel against something!'

'Hey. This is me you're talking about.' Ruth was laughing. 'Honest, Mum, I didn't mean anything about your cooking.'

'I know, love,' Bea told her, aware that she had over-reacted and even more aware why. She had spent a lonely evening regretting her stubborn pride which had prevented her from accepting Liam's invitation to go with them.

She abandoned her pointless pondering on what might have been to tune into their conversation. Ruth and Liam were talking about a newly released film which had caused a storm of protest over its horrific contents.

'I won't be going to see it,' Liam said. 'I've seen the grim result of too many accidents in A and E to want to go and see gore on the screen. I don't call that enjoyment.'

'I bet you won't go with me either.' Ruth turned to her mother.

'Too right. If you want nightmares you can go and see it with your friends once you get to university.'

'Thanks a bunch,' she muttered.

Having finished his coffee, Liam stood. 'I must be going. I'll see you both on Monday, no doubt. Thank you for rescuing me from my horrible digs for another evening.'

Recalling her decision, Bea hesitated then said, 'About your digs, Liam.'

He frowned. 'Yes?'

'Have you told them you're leaving?'

'Yes. Why?'

'I...er, I...'

'You've let your spare room to someone else?' he finished for her.

She knew her cheeks were flaming as her eyes were caught and held by his. 'No. it's...it's not that, but—'

'There's no problem, then. See you both.' With an amused curl of his lips, he winked at Ruth and made his way to the front door.

Aware that he had guessed her intention to withdraw her offer, he hadn't given her the opportunity. Resolving to tell him in private first thing on Monday morning, she followed him to the door.

'Goodnight, Bea.' He leaned towards her and she thought he was going to kiss her, until he looked over her shoulder and must have seen Ruth hovering in the kitchen doorway. 'Goodnight, Ruth.' He strode away without a backward glance.

Bea locked up and turned to find Ruth standing behind her.

'Honestly, Mum. What are you playing at? Don't tell me you're still not sure about Liam moving in?'

Bea coloured.

Ruth was exasperated. 'What's got into you?'

Bea groaned.

'Ruth, love, it's barely a week since he joined the practice. We don't really know him and it's silly to rush things.'

'I told you—you're becoming an old stick-in-the-mud. You need to get out and meet a few more people.'

Bea sat motionless for several moments after she'd gone. Was she foolish, trying to distance herself from Liam? It would be so easy to embark on an affair with him for the short time he was in Bargate, but it would be insane. Wouldn't it? Even though a resultant pregnancy wouldn't be an issue this time, it would do little for either her or her daughter's well-being. Especially as Ruth seemed to be treating him like the father she'd never known.

Her chaotic thoughts were disturbed by Ruth's CD player blaring at an unacceptable level for that time of night. Bea sighed and climbed the stairs to knock on her door, before making her way to bed. But not to sleep. She spent a restless night with her thoughts, before getting up in time for the early morning church service.

It seemed as if all hell was let loose the moment Bea and Ruth arrived at the health centre on Monday morning. There was standing-room-only in the waiting room, a queue at the reception desk and it seemed like every telephone in the place was ringing.

'What's happening?' Bea asked the practice manager as they managed to get through the crowds to the rear of the reception desk.

'Didn't you hear the news this morning? A case of Legionnaires' disease was admitted to the local hospital yesterday. He's in his late seventies and is critically ill. The media have blown the situation up out of all proportion, saying hundreds could be affected.'

'Do they know where he might have contracted it?' Bea asked.

Mair shook her head. 'That's the problem. The chap on the radio was pointing the finger at the cooling systems of every large building in the town, including the hospital! He could have caught it anywhere. Goodness knows where he might have been in the last ten days. The authorities are certainly not saying.'

Liam had come up as she finished speaking. 'We'll probably never know, unless there are more cases confirmed.'

Ruth, who had been listening intently to what was being said, asked, 'What exactly is Legionnaires' disease?'

Liam told her, 'It's a kind of pneumonia and is much more serious in the elderly, which makes it a little easier to work out a plan of action. Katy's been besieged with telephone callers of all ages, demanding urgent appointments.

'When they can't get one, they ring back with a request for a home visit. We're inundated already. If there were forty-eight hours in the day we wouldn't get round them all.'

'I'm just about to ring John and ask him to come in to help,' Mair told them, and scurried away.

'What do you want me to do?'

'Alicia's been monitoring the calls. It seemed that nearly everybody on our books is feverish today and has a flu-like illness with headaches, muscular pains and a cough.'

'The symptoms mentioned on the radio?'

Liam grinned. 'You've got it. Many even have upset stomachs! What's new after the weekend?'

Alicia joined them. 'They've all made their own diagnosis and want it confirmed. We need someone able to reassure them to take the calls at the moment. Someone with medical knowledge. I've patients waiting now, but if you could hold the fort until John gets in, Bea, that would be great.'

'What time's the first treatment-room appointment?' Liam was frowning.

Bea consulted the diaries. 'Nine-fifteen. They'll just have to wait or rebook. Perhaps Katy and Ruth can explain to them when they arrive.'

'John's on his way,' Mair called across to him.

'Thank goodness for that.' Liam walked across to speak to Mair where they couldn't be overheard, and Bea followed.

'Perhaps when he arrives you'd ask him to contact the environmental medical officer and see if there's anything definite about the source.'

Mair nodded and returned to her office. Bea joined Ruth and Katy behind the reception desk. As she took her seat at the back, she noticed Ruth's stricken face. 'Don't worry, love. The dust'll soon settle and we'll be back to normal.'

'Will we have lots of patients affected?'

Bea shook her head. 'If we're lucky we won't have one.'

Ruth and Katy didn't manage to persuade even one person on Bea's list to change their appointment, so she was glad when she saw John arrive.

'Sorry about this, John, but if you don't mind I'll start my list now. If you need to get away, just give a shout.'

He smiled ruefully. 'My mates'll have teed off without me by now, so I might as well stay.' He nodded towards the window. 'Wouldn't this just happen on the best Monday weather for weeks?'

Bea called her first patient through. Although she worked throughout her lunch-hour, she never caught up and her afternoon appointments ran into the evening.

When Ruth was ready to leave, she came in search of Bea. 'I'll get the meal ready. When do you think you'll be home?'

'Sevenish, I should say. Do you want to take the car?'

Ruth shook her head. 'I'll bus it tonight.'

Apart from John telling her that no source had been found, Bea hadn't seen any of the doctors that day. They had been too bogged down with the house calls and the extra appointments.

Tuesday and Wednesday were very similar, although the rush of worried patients *was* gradually diminishing.

So when, during her Thursday afternoon diabetic clinic, Bert Lane, one of her more stable diabetics, said he was having problems controlling his sugar levels, Bea had plenty of time to discuss what he'd been eating and drinking.

When he revealed nothing that could account for the swing in levels, she said, 'You're perhaps incubating a mild infection. A cold probably.'

'Funny you should say that,' he said. 'I thought I had a touch of flu these last few days, but I think I must be fighting it off.'

He described how his muscles had been aching and told her he hadn't been able to get the temperature right in his sheltered housing. 'One minute I'm hot, the next I'm shivery. I feel better today, apart from the head-ache.'

'Any cough?'

He laughed sheepishly. 'I always have, being as I smoke and shouldn't.'

'But no sickness, you said.'

'No. Stomach's too strong for that.'

Bea checked his temperature and pulse and, finding both raised, noted that he was breathing rather rapidly.

'I think we'll get a doctor to have a listen to your chest, Bert. You might need an antibiotic.'

'I shouldn't think so. Just some bug doing the rounds.'

Although Bert was trying to make light of it, there was something about his condition that made her uneasy. It *could* be just a chest infection, as he'd said, but she couldn't dismiss a persistent niggle at the back of her mind that queried if he could be suffering from Legionnaires' disease.

If she hadn't heard about the other case on Monday, she wouldn't have given it a thought, but now she wanted Bert checked out.

She rang Reception. 'Any doctors in?'

Ruth answered. 'Liam's just gone into his room.'

Bea asked Bert to wait where he was and took his notes and her records across to Liam.

When he called her in, she said, 'I'm probably being silly, but I wonder if you'd take a look at Mr Lane. He's feverish and generally unwell, and his sugar levels are somewhat out of control. Unusual for him.'

'And?'

'And what?'

'There's something you're not saying, isn't there?'

Could he read her that well? 'I just wondered if he might have Legionnaires' disease. His breathing's rapid and he's coughing but, then, he is a smoker so you'll probably laugh me out of the treatment room. But I'm just not happy about him.'

'Don't put yourself down, Bea. Intuition is one of the best reasons for further investigation I know. Let's take a look at him.'

When Liam had questioned and examined Bert very thoroughly, he told him, 'I think I'd like to take some blood and perhaps get an X-ray done on that chest. I'll go and see what I can arrange. Just you wait there.'

Bea followed him back to his own room.

He gave a deep sigh. 'I'm afraid you might be right, Bea. I'll give the hospital a bell and hope they'll agree to admit him. A diabetic smoker living on his own is a poor risk, if that's what it is. I'd rather he was under twenty-four-hour care for the moment, at least until a diagnosis is made.'

'I've a couple more diabetics to see. Can I put him back in the waiting room?'

'Use Alicia's room if you don't mind.' She started to open the door. 'And, Bea?'

'Yes?'

'Well done.'

She felt at least ten feet tall as she went in search of her notes for the last two patients on her list. 'Dr Taylor will be with you in a moment,' she told Bert. 'OK?'

He nodded and Bea gave him a reassuring smile. A smile that she found difficult to wipe from her face for the remainder of the afternoon. It was very satisfying to know that even if she wasn't right, Liam hadn't dismissed her suspicions out of hand.

When the time came for her to leave, Liam was still not sure if the hospital was going to admit Bert Lane. 'They're inundated with patients, as we are. It's a case of deciding who they can discharge before they can take him.'

'Shall I get him something to eat and drink?'

'Does he have his insulin with him?'

'I shouldn't imagine so.'

Liam was about to speak when his telephone rang. It was obviously a message he'd been waiting for and, after thanking the caller, he replaced the receiver with a smile.

'A bed for Bert. On ward twenty-six. But not until seven. Probably best if he goes home and takes his usual insulin and food. Meanwhile, I'll try and arrange transport to the hospital for him.' As he lifted the receiver, he checked his watch and groaned. 'It's after five. I bet I'm too late.'

There was obviously no reply and Bea said, 'I'm finished now and Ruth's working late. I'll take him home and then collect him just before seven.'

'I don't think you should, in case he's infectious.'

She shrugged. 'I've been in the treatment room with him for the last hour or so. If I was going to catch it I would have done so by now. And it's not that infectious to healthy nurses, is it?'

Liam shook his head. 'What would this place do without you? And we haven't given another thought to getting you some help.'

She laughed. 'I shouldn't think you've had a chance this week!'

'Maybe not, but I'll make a point of seeing John about it again tomorrow.'

'My hero,' she joshed with a grin.

She picked up Bert's records and the letter Liam had scribbled for the hospital and opened the door. 'It looks like your patients are starting to arrive for evening surgery.'

He nodded. 'Katy said so when she put that call through. I'll come back with you first and have a word with Bert.'

Bea went back to the treatment room and quickly tidied while Liam told Bert what was happening.

'What do you think it might be?'

'Possibly some kind of an infection, but until the sugar levels stabilise you'll be better off in hospital where it's easier to get any necessary tests done.'

He explained what Bea had offered to do and, after clapping him on the shoulder and wishing him luck, he left her to get on with it while he tackled his over-full list.

She was about to accompany Bert out to her car when he told her he needed to visit the loo.

While she waited her thoughts turned to Liam. As he'd left her room she'd remembered she hadn't had the time or the opportunity to tell him about not wanting him as a lodger, They'd been so busy she hadn't given it another thought. And nearly another week had slipped by. But it would have been churlish to do so when he was so busy that he didn't have time to go out and look for something else. Wouldn't it?

She felt herself on the two prongs of a dilemma. Her fear had been that she was so aware of his sexual chemistry that she didn't think she could remain just a friend if they were living under the same roof, and now she didn't think they would remain friends at all if she asked him to look for somewhere else to live at this short notice. And that wouldn't be good for their working relationship. Would it?

Perhaps it would work. That first week they'd seen

so much of one another that she'd thought there was no way she would be able to cope and had panicked.

It had been much easier this week. Perhaps it was just that he'd known no one else in the area when he'd first arrived. Once he had time to make other friends there would be no problem. Or would there?

She was so busy weighing the two sides of her argument that she didn't immediately notice Bert returning. When his footsteps did jolt her out of her attempt to come to a decision, she leapt to her feet and with a smile asked, 'Ready?'

He nodded, and as they walked out to the car he asked, 'That new doctor causing you grief, Sister?'

'Dr Taylor? No. What on earth made you say that?'

He chuckled. 'You just wasn't your usual self when he came and told me you'd see me right. And you were so pensive when I came back I thought he must have upset you.'

'No, nothing like that. I just have a problem I was trying to decide how to resolve.'

'It's not caused by you taking me to the hospital when you should be home, is it?'

She gave him a reassuring smile. 'No. Nothing like that. I'd be going home to an empty house, I'll still be home before my daughter.'

'That's OK, then. As long as you don't mind. I could always get a taxi, see.'

'I'm going to visit someone at the hospital anyway.'

He seemed happier to know that, and as they were already at his sheltered home by that time, she arranged to pick him up an hour later.

She had little time for any more thought as she rushed home, prepared a casserole for Ruth and herself to eat later and set it to cook, before going back to collect him.

She delivered him to ward twenty-six. After saying they'd keep in touch, she telephoned the orthopaedic department and asked about Sharon's progress.

Despite her reassurance to Bert, she decided not to visit that day in case she was harbouring any infection that an under-par Sharon could contract.

'She's doing very well now. Great friends with the lady in the next bed who's very good to her.'

'I'm glad to hear it. Give her my love and say I'll try and pop in later in the week.'

Liam rang later that evening and asked how she had got on.

'Fine, thanks. Bert seemed happy enough to be admitted, and apparently we wouldn't believe the change in Sharon!'

'Has she restarted her radiotherapy treatment?'

'I didn't ask. I'm sorry, Liam. I never gave it a thought.'

'Not to worry,' he assured her. 'I'll check with the oncology centre tomorrow. Just to make sure she isn't forgotten.'

'Right.'

'By the way, I reminded John this evening about another nurse. He's already been working on figures and need and is going to raise the subject at a practice meeting tomorrow. Time permitting!'

'I'll look forward to hearing what he has to say.'

Bea was thoughtful as she replaced the receiver a few moments later. There had been no need for Liam to ring. Everything they'd discussed could have waited until the next morning, so why had he taken the trouble?

Was it just his genuine interest in everyone he came

into contact with? Or had he been at a loose end and wanted a chat? She couldn't really believe that a man so full of *bonhomie* and sexual magnetism would be on his own for long, wherever he chose to settle.

'Who was that?' Ruth was watching her with curiosity.

'Liam. He wanted to know how I'd got on at the hospital.'

'Is he coming round?'

'No.'

Ruth shrugged. 'So why are you standing there like an idiot? What else did he say?'

'Would you believe, "Goodnight"?'

'Wonderful,' Ruth breathed.

As Ruth was on the early shift she travelled in with Bea the next morning. They were approaching the health centre by the time she overcame her early morning lethargy sufficiently to ask, 'Have you any plans for the weekend, Mum?'

'Apart from the early morning surgery, no. Why do you ask?'

'I wondered—'

She didn't get any further with what she thought because, while Bea was indicating to turn from the other side of the road into the car park, Liam's car swung out of it at speed, squealing a trail of hot rubber from the tyres.

'What the…?' shrieked Ruth as it turned into the road and swung in a wide arc, heading straight for the Fiesta.

Bea frantically tried to move out of the way, but the traffic going her way was so heavy there was nowhere to go. Somehow the car missed them by centimetres. It took her several moments before she could pull herself together and persuade her trembling legs to mobilise themselves.

She turned into the parking space just inside the gate, switched off the engine, slumped over the wheel and demanded in a muffled voice, 'What the hell did he think he was doing?'

'Are you all right, Mum?'

She looked up at her daughter's concerned face, her eyes wet with tears. 'Just about. No thanks to Liam Taylor.'

'It wasn't Liam driving, Mum.'

'It wasn't? Who was it, then?'

'I don't know.' Ruth moved away and opened the passenger door to speak to Liam who was running across the car park towards them.

'What's happened, Liam?'

He didn't answer but put his head in through the passenger door and asked anxiously, 'Are you all right, Bea? I saw what happened. Bloody idiot.'

'What happened?'

'He stole my car. Mair's alerted the police. My bag was in it.'

Bea climbed from behind the wheel. Liam raced round to the other side of the car and took a firm hold of her arm. 'Looks like he frightened you witless.'

'You can say that again. How he missed us I'll never know.'

His arm encircling her tenderly, Liam helped her through to the staffroom, calling to Katy on the way, 'Get me a cab. I must get off on this visit.' He took a record card out of his pocket to check the address.

Bea handed him her keys. 'Take the Fiesta. It'll just be sitting there all day.'

Liam looked as if he was about to refuse, then smiled

and said, 'Thanks.' Then he raced from the building, this time calling to Katy to forget about the cab.

She was so shaken that everything seemed to take longer that morning. She was so busy she neither set eyes on Liam nor heard anything about his car.

It was nearly one when she had enough time to ask Ruth if there was any news.

'Not really. The chap who took it has been hanging about for days, apparently. He came in with Cilla Jenkins earlier in the week. He just seized the opportunity when Liam popped in for Mrs Guyler's record card.'

'He left the car unlocked?' Bea queried incredulously.

'I don't think so—but he left his bag in there, something he never does usually, but he was only going to be a minute.'

Bea groaned. 'Poor Liam.'

Katy, who had been eavesdropping, chuckled. 'He was using the surgery's spare bag as well, so he's having to do his visits with just his stethoscope and a prescription pad! That'll teach him.'

'By the way, Mum, Liam rang in and asked if you needed the car at all and I told him not until five. Hope that was OK.'

Bea nodded. She only had a couple of dressings to redo that afternoon so she spent the rest of the time checking and re-ordering her stores after the hectic week they'd had.

Liam came in search of her at four. 'I'm sorry to have kept the car so long. What a day!'

'No news of your own car?'

Liam grimaced. 'Burnt out. Down by the river. They've got the chap and the bag. Drugs all missing,

of course, but what was in there won't be of much use
to him, or his pal, Cilla Jenkins.'

'You think *she* was involved?'

He shrugged. 'Someone's got them—the police
couldn't find them in his pad. But they found plenty of
other things.'

'Drugs?'

'Funnily enough, no, but what they suspect are the
proceeds of several recent robberies. Probably needed
the money to buy Cilla all that rough cider!' he joked
grimly.

'Cilla should have ditched him long ago.'

'In my experience a woman who thinks she's in love
can't tell the difference between good and bad in a
man.'

He said it so bitterly that Bea recoiled. 'That's a bit
of a generalisation, isn't it?'

Liam shrugged angrily. 'It's what I believe.' He held
out her car keys.

Bea didn't move. She was too busy trying to work
out what could have happened in his past to cause him
to react so vehemently. It was in such sharp contrast to
his usual gentle manner that she believed he must have
some very good reason. She wondered if it could have
some connection to his admission that he'd had no parents to support him through university.

He must have recognised her bewilderment at his behaviour. 'That was unforgivable, Bea. It might have
been a God-awful day but that's no reason for me to
take it out on you.'

'Forget it. Would you like to keep the car for now?'

He shook his head. 'You need it to get home.'

'Can't you hire one for the time being?'

'I was going to, but I'd arranged to visit a friend

tomorrow, and when I rang to say I wouldn't be able to make it, she said it was pointless me buying one for the short time until I went abroad. She isn't using hers at the moment. I'm just on my way to ring about train times.'

Intrigued by someone offering him a car for that length of time, Bea murmured, 'That's very generous. Where is the car?'

'That's the only problem. It's just this side of Manchester.'

Bea thought for a moment, then offered impetuously. 'I'm on duty in the morning, but I could drive you to pick it up later.' Perhaps this was a way to learn more about him.

'That's hardly fair on your weekend, Bea.'

'I don't have anything planned.'

'What about Ruth?'

Remembering his comments about her needing to let Ruth go, she muttered, 'We don't live in one another's pockets *all* the time, Liam. Once she finally falls out of bed, I expect she'll hit the shops with her friends.'

'I know exactly what that means,' he told her rue-fully. 'My feet never touched the ground last Saturday.'

'Serves you right—' She bit back the end of the sentence she'd started. It really wouldn't be diplomatic to imply he was too old to keep up with younger people!

'I enjoy driving and honestly don't mind in the least.' If the truth were told, the driving wasn't the only thing she would enjoy. Being with Liam and learning more about him was an attraction in itself. Stupid under the circumstances, but she couldn't help herself.

'If you're sure, it *would* be marvellous. What time would you like to leave?'

'Twelve-thirtyish all right? That would give me time for a bit of shopping as well.'

'Fine. I'll ring Jenny and I'm sure she'll get us a meal before you set off back.'

'That sounds good.' She wasn't at all sure she meant it. It depended how close a friend Jenny was! 'Will you be driving back Saturday evening as well?'

He shook his head. 'No. I'll be staying the night. I'd intended going up there this weekend anyway.'

Of course he was staying the night! It would need to be someone as close as that to lend him the car. As she walked back to the treatment room she realised what a fool she was. If he and this Jenny meant so much to one another, she could just as easily come down to collect him for the weekend. Couldn't she? What on earth must he think of her rash offer? No doubt when he told Jenny about her they would have a good laugh at the poor frustrated single mother who had nothing better to do with her weekend.

CHAPTER SEVEN

IT WAS too late now. She could hardly withdraw the offer. Bea supposed it was a major trait in her character to try and give a helping hand whenever she could.

She remembered Liam's bitterness when he'd said a woman who believed she was in love couldn't recognise a bad character when she saw one.

What was he thinking of her at this moment? That she had made the impetuous offer because she thought herself in love with him? Why else would anyone give up their Saturday? She felt the colour rush to her cheeks at the thought.

One thing was for sure—she'd intended to offer to run him home that evening after his surgery, but there was no way she was going to now, so the sooner she left the better. She rang through to Reception and told Ruth she was leaving on the stroke of five if she wanted a lift.

She could hear surprise in Ruth's voice as she asked, 'What about Liam? How will he get home?'

'John or Alicia will probably take him. Otherwise he can get a taxi. I'm not his personal chauffeur, am I?'

Her abrupt outburst was met by an unaccustomed silence from Ruth, followed by a refusal of her offer. 'I don't think I can get away by five, so I'll make my own way home.'

Unwilling to face Liam until she got her thoughts sorted out, Bea locked up her cupboards and left the health centre as fast as she could.

* * *

'Mum, you remember I was asking about your weekend plans when that chap nearly hit us with Liam's car this morning?'

Bea paused in serving out their evening meal.

'Ye-es?'

'I was going to say, if you weren't using the car could I drive up to Stafford and see Lisa?'

'What for?'

'Just a visit. You know she started this job up there? Well, she's settled into her flat now and has asked me to go and see it.'

'You've never done such a long journey on your own before.'

'I've got to do it some time. I'd go up and back in daylight. I promise I'd be careful.' The last sentence was a wheedling plea.

Bea smiled. 'I know you would, love, but I'm using the car tomorrow.' Ruth's face fell. 'But as it happens, I'm running Liam up to Manchester to pick up a car, so I *could* drop you on the way and pick you up on the journey back.'

'Could you, Mum? That would be super.' She frowned. 'Why's he getting a car from Manchester?'

'A friend has offered to lend him one until he goes abroad.'

'Some friend!' Ruth exclaimed. 'I wish I had one like that.'

Bea nodded ruefully. 'He certainly seems to have a way with him that prompts people to go out of their way to do things for him. Look at me. I lent him the Fiesta today and have offered to drive him all that way tomorrow. Don't ask me why.'

Ruth nodded thoughtfully. 'He has this knack of attracting everyone's sympathy. I suppose that's why

John suggested he move into my room when he knew his digs were so awful.'

Bea smiled at her daughter. Ruth was growing up fast.

The decision about the trip to Manchester had been made for her by Ruth the previous evening.

She really wouldn't have wanted Ruth driving all that way on her own. OK, perhaps she was over-protective, but this seemed the ideal solution, so perhaps it had been meant that she'd made the offer to Liam the day before.

She was late leaving the surgery so decided to forgo the shopping as she and Ruth wouldn't be at home all day. Ruth had made sandwiches for their lunch, and there was just time to consume them before they set off to pick up Liam.

He was in a jovial mood, and when he saw Ruth he teased, 'She couldn't do without you after all?'

Annoyed, Bea retorted, 'She's going to visit her friend who has moved to Stafford. She's not a very experienced driver so it's a good opportunity for her to get some practice in. She'll do this part of the journey.'

Liam pretended to be horrified. 'You mean I'm entrusting my life to a novice driver? I'd better check my life insurance is up to date.'

Ruth rose to his bait. 'I'm not that much of a novice. I just haven't had the chance to do long journeys.'

Bea felt the need to defend her. 'She's a very good driver. I'm quite happy for her to drive.'

Liam looked at her oddly, then climbed into the rear seat, saying quietly as he did so, 'I was only joking, Bea.'

Bea wished again that she'd never made this offer.

She would be much happier relaxing at home than sharing the company of a man who thought her over-protective of her daughter *and* a romantic idiot to boot. If she could have thought of a way to get out of the journey at that moment she would certainly have done so.

Ruth drove in silence until she was on the motorway, then broke the awkward silence by saying in her usual outspoken fashion, 'I said to Mum that your friend must think a lot of you to lend you her car.'

'She does.'

'So why doesn't she need it at the moment?' Ruth probed, obviously as keen as Bea was to learn more, but less inhibited.

'Because she's recently undergone a hip replacement operation and is content for her husband to drive her around for the time being.'

After Bea's imaginings of the past sixteen hours, she was hard pressed to stifle a gasp. Liam wasn't fooled.

'Something the matter, Bea?'

'Er...no,' she protested in a strangled voice. 'It was just that, well, just that...' Searching for words, she ground to a halt.

'Just that?' he prompted.

'I don't know. I suppose I thought it was someone younger.' She knew her colour was rising and so didn't turn to look at him.

'*I* didn't give you that impression, did I?'

Bea shook her head. 'You know how it is. We all jump to conclusions.'

Ruth was overtaking and Bea, sensing tension rising between Liam and herself, sought to diffuse it before it affected Ruth's concentration. 'Have you got any directions in Stafford, Bea?'

'Yep. We come off the motorway and head for the town. As we come into the built-up area, it's a road to the left.' Ruth retrieved a piece of paper from the dashboard. 'That's the name of the road. She says we can't miss the house. It's on the corner and painted bright green and yellow! It's been converted into flats for students.'

After they'd dropped Ruth off, and Bea had arranged to pick her up between seven and eight, Liam offered to drive. 'It's only fair. You have the journey back.'

Bea would have preferred to drive. She wasn't looking forward to being alone in the car with him and could have pretended she was engrossed in the traffic if the conversation became threatening.

However, she handed over the keys and they didn't speak until they were back on the motorway.

Liam relaxed and turned to smile at her. 'The traffic's not too bad, is it? Thank goodness we're not going the other way.'

'Next week it'll be like that in this direction, with the first batch of holidaymakers returning.'

'I guess so. What a daft system it is that decrees everyone should take their holiday within the space of six weeks.'

Bea laughed. 'And have it run from Saturday to Saturday. It's like the rush hour. The starting day of holidays should be staggered.'

'Sounds good, but it would hit the pockets of the traders. If I vacated the house on Monday and the next tenants didn't come until Friday, that's four days' money lost.'

'I suppose so.'

'What do you and Ruth do for your holidays?'

'When she was very small, I took her for days out. Now she goes to stay with Mum and Dad in Portishead.'

'And you?'

'I stay for the weekend, both when I take her and collect her.'

'And in between?'

'It's an opportunity to get on with all those jobs I never get round to.'

'No wonder Ruth thinks you ought to travel.'

'Does she?'

'Have you never thought about working abroad?'

'Before I left school I did. We were all full of ambitious plans in those days. Not many of us realised them.'

'So you wouldn't like to see something of the world?'

'Maybe some time. But not until Ruth has finished at university.'

Surprisingly he dropped the subject, and instead observed, 'You thought I was borrowing the car from a girlfriend?'

'As much as I thought about it, I suppose I did.' Bea was hedging and she soon realised Liam knew it.

'Do I detect a note of censure in your voice?'

'No, I—' Bea started to defend herself, but he wasn't listening.

'I suppose you also think that's why I keep moving on. That I love 'em and leave 'em.' His tone was increasingly bitter. 'If you can't trust me, I wonder you're allowing me to move into your house. Perhaps you'd prefer it if, after all, I don't?'

'Of course I trust you. It's just that—that—' She searched for words that would explain how she felt, without giving too much away.

'You're suddenly faced with decisions to make without Ruth's need of you to hide behind?'

Startled by his clear perception, she murmured, 'I suppose…it's just that everything in my life seems to be changing at the same time.'

Before he could probe for details, she reverted to their earlier conversation. 'Before we get there, it would be nice to know who these people are I'm going to meet. Are they family?'

'I have no relatives. Jenny and Stan were foster-parents.' It was an unemotional statement of fact that warned Bea it wasn't a subject he was ready to enlarge on.

'I look forward to meeting them. They sound a generous couple.'

'They are.' His eyes were fixed firmly on the road ahead, but there was an edge to his voice that told her it was time to change the subject again. She obviously *wasn't* the only one with hang-ups!

'I've never been this far north before. I expected rows and rows of houses, not green fields.'

Liam was turning the car off the motorway and he laughed.

'I diagnose too much *Coronation Street*! Cheshire is a beautiful county. A little more built up towards Manchester, I grant you, but the village we're going to is as attractive as any of your Cotswold ones.'

'I didn't mean to be rude! I just had no idea.'

'I wish there was time to show you Chester. Now, there's a city I could live in.'

He pulled up in front of a half-timbered house built on the periphery of what was obviously the village green. Although it was quite a modern construction, it blended in well with its older neighbours.

'What a great place to live!'

'You can say that again.' He opened the boot of her car and retrieved his overnight bag, then handed her the keys. 'Come and meet Jen and Stan.'

The front door was already open, and when he'd kissed them both, he introduced Bea.

Stanley's smile of welcome was warm and Jenny gave Bea a hug. 'Lovely to meet you. Come in, and make yourself at home.'

'Cup of tea?' she asked once they were seated in the chintz-decorated living room.

Bea nodded her agreement as Liam replied in a voice she was amused to notice was already slipping into a northern accent, 'I could murder one.'

'Good journey?' Stan asked as he motioned for Jenny to sit down and let him get the tea.

'No hold-ups at all. I just hope Bea won't encounter some on the way back. There was quite a trail of holiday traffic heading south.'

When she had poured the tea, Jenny apologised for not offering scones or cake as she usually would have. 'But we've timed our meal for fivish and I don't want to take the edge off your appetite.'

'You're doing incredibly well, Jenny. I hope you're not overdoing it.' Liam had become the concerned professional. 'No problems with the op at all?'

She shook her head. 'I can't describe what it's like to have relief from that constant pain. I feel ready to go for a ten-mile hike.'

He smiled. 'Knowing you, I expect you will! But not yet. Give your new hip a chance.'

'I will. I promise I'm doing exactly what I'm told and Stan's been marvellous. Waiting on me hand and foot!'

Liam looked from one to the other fondly. 'He's even doing the gardening, is he?'

'No way.' They all laughed, leaving Bea feeling excluded from some private joke.

'Sorry.' Liam turned to her. 'Stan hates gardening and if Jenny does let him loose in it, he pulls up her precious plants and leaves the weeds.'

'Best strategy out if you don't want to get asked again.' He laughed. 'Young Liam never learned. He always tried to do everything right and got landed with all the dirty work.'

'I enjoyed it,' he protested defensively.

They all laughed then Liam asked, 'Would you like to see Jenny's handiwork, Bea? The garden should be looking its best about now.'

'I would indeed.'

'Good. Then we can put the finishing touches to the meal and set the table.' Jenny gave Stan a knowing wink and Bea felt colour start to tinge her cheeks.

It was obvious they were being pushed out into the garden to give them time alone together, leaving Bea with the uncomfortable impression that they thought she was something more than the work colleague Liam had introduced her as.

Unless...unless he'd said something of the sort when he'd rung them the day before? But why should he? No. They had probably just put two and two together and made five.

She admired the layout of the garden, then went to examine the labels attached to the shrubs lining the path.

'Are you a gardener?'

'I try but don't really know what I'm doing. Luckily, it's only a small square patch at the back.'

'Perhaps I can help when I move in.'

She laughed. 'You can take it over if you like. There's not really room enough for two of us to work in it.'

'That's a pity.' Thinking he was joking at her offering a let-out, she swung round to tease him about chickening out already, but their gazes locked and held for long enough for her to recognise he meant it.

He raised an eyebrow and said in a suggestively soft voice that sent an anticipatory shudder through her, 'Gardening together might have been fun.'

'I'm not sure I'm in your league, though.'

'As a gardener, or…'

He left her to fill in her own alternative, but as she wasn't sure herself exactly what she had meant she shrugged. 'Stan implied you're a perfectionist. I'm not. As long as it looks tidy, that's good enough for me.'

He shook his head. 'Having seen you at work, I can't believe that.'

Jenny called at that moment. 'Come on in, you two. Grub up.'

The casserole Jenny and Stan had made between them was delicious, and Jenny was such a beguiling extrovert that it was impossible not to be drawn into the conversation.

Bea guessed it would be impossible for anyone not to get on with Jenny, and she was even wishing her own mother had been more like that when Stan proudly served the trifle concocted by him alone—something her own father would never have attempted. It was truly delicious and a fitting finale to a most enjoyable meal.

While Stan and Liam cleared the dishes, Bea popped up to the bathroom. On her return she allowed Jenny to persuade her they didn't need to help. 'We can have a good old gossip instead.'

Bea sank onto the settee with her mug of coffee, replete and relaxed, hating the thought of climbing back into her Fiesta alone.

'It's been lovely to see you both today,' Jenny told her.

Unsuspectingly, Bea replied, 'I've really enjoyed it, too.'

'Once Ruth has gone off to university you must both come up again and stay the night. I know Liam would love to show you the area.'

Recalling the way Jenny had pushed them off into the garden alone, Bea tried to disabuse her of the idea that she was there as Liam's girlfriend. 'I only came today because Liam needed a lift.'

'I know that, and I can understand you wanting to spend as much time with Ruth as you can, but in September it'll be different. You'll have nothing to keep you at home.'

Bea sighed. Jenny was telling her nothing she didn't already know, but she was assuming much that wasn't true. 'Jenny, Liam and I—'

'You're going to Malaysia with him. Is that it?' Jenny wasn't giving Bea a chance to explain.

'No. I want to be here for Ruth if she needs me. Jenny, about Liam and me—'

Jenny leaned across and patted her hand. 'You expected me to be upset at him finding someone new?' The tears sparkling in her eyes belied her next words, which left an already confused Bea totally so. 'I've come to terms with the situation now and just want Liam to be happy.'

What on earth was she talking about? Was this something she thought a girlfriend of Liam's would know about? In that case, the sooner Bea put her right about the situation, the better.

'Jenny—'

She was interrupted again, this time by Stan and Liam rejoining them.

Jenny looked up at them with a wan smile. 'We've been having a real heart-to-heart. I like this girl, Liam.'

Bea saw apprehension flash across Liam's face the moment he saw the tears in Jenny's eyes.

'What have you been talking about?' he asked suspiciously.

'I said next time you come Bea must stay the night as well. Then you can show her around.'

He nodded. 'I'd like to do that. Very much.'

Stan asked Bea if she knew Chester, and any opportunity to find out what on earth Jenny had been talking about was lost as they launched into a discussion of the city's heritage.

Bea checked her watch and saw that if she was to pick up Ruth and get home at a reasonable hour, it was time to leave.

'I really must go. Thank you again for your hospitality and the lovely meal. It's been great to meet you both.'

Jenny and Stan remained at the door, and Liam accompanied her to the Fiesta.

'You can remember the way to the motorway?'

She nodded.

'Thanks for bringing me, Bea. I hope it's been a pleasant day for you.'

She nodded. 'I've enjoyed meeting them both.' Although she was bursting with questions, she couldn't ask them with Jenny and Stan watching.

'Drive carefully.' He leaned over and, before kissing her gently on the lips, said softly, 'I'm sorry if Jenny's said anything she shouldn't. We'll talk on Monday.'

He stepped back, leaving her even more confused but acutely aware of his kiss, which, she told herself, had been purely for his foster-parents' benefit.

Her journey to Stafford was accompanied by unanswered questions circling round and round in her mind. What had Jenny been talking about? Why hadn't Liam mentioned it if there was a possibility she would? Was it something he had to hide? Was it something that should make her think twice about taking him into her own home? Was it something that made him a threat to Ruth?

As she turned off the motorway to pick up Ruth, she realised that she didn't want to believe any of the crazy ideas forming in response to her relentless interrogation.

And that could only mean one thing. Although she had made a conscious decision not to become involved, her subconscious was urging her to ignore that resolve. Whenever she was near Liam, his maleness threatened to overpower her rationality. Not to put too fine a point on it, she was so aroused by his masculinity that she was in danger of falling hopelessly in love with him. Something she must avoid at all costs.

When she reached the door Ruth had disappeared through earlier, Lisa flung it open. 'She's just paying a last-minute call to the loo.'

'Have you had a good day?' Bea asked.

'Fabulous. We haven't stopped talking. I've heard all about this dishy doctor of yours.'

'Liam? He's only with us for a short time.'

'Going to work abroad, Ruth said?'

Bea nodded, relieved to see Ruth approaching down

the hall. At this moment Liam Taylor was the last person she wanted to discuss.

After Ruth and Lisa had exchanged extravagant farewells, Bea led the way to the car.

'Are you driving?'

'I don't think I'd better. I had a glass of wine.'

Bea slid behind the wheel and they were soon back on the motorway, with Ruth chattering non-stop about her day and Lisa's new life.

They were nearly home when she asked about Liam. 'Did you find any skeletons in his cupboard?'

Bea realised she didn't know. 'I met his foster-parents. They were super people. I think he was very lucky to find them.'

'Did you discover what happened to his parents?'

'I didn't try to.'

'Why ever not? I would've.'

'I know you would,' Bea said with a laugh, 'but I'm not so insensitive.'

'You didn't have to ask *him*.'

'Let's say the opportunity didn't arise.'

Ruth gave her a sidelong look. 'You didn't enjoy your day?'

'That's not what I said—'

'No, but—'

'I was only there for a short time. Just long enough to see the garden and eat a meal. You can't walk in on people you've never met before and ask personal questions.'

'I suppose not.'

Hating the edginess creeping into their exchange, Bea asked, 'What was Lisa's flat like?'

'Ugh! She calls it a flat but it's nothing more than a squalid room. And not my idea of comfort at all. If that's what passes for student accommodation, I'm glad I've a place in the hall of residence.'

Bea laughed. 'You've been spoilt, my girl. Totally spoilt. I don't expect the rooms in hall will be that much better.'

Ruth sniffed. 'If I have to put up with a room like that I'll come back home. Pronto! Even if you have moved Liam into my room!'

'I don't think that's likely. He seems happy enough to move into the spare one.'

'I suppose after today you must know a lot more about him.'

Bea was thoughtful. 'You know, I'm not sure that I do…'

'You are happier about him moving in, though?'

'I think so. Why do you ask?'

'I dunno. When we talk about him you always appear…'

'Appear what?' Bea prompted sharply.

'Well, defensive, I suppose I'd call it. As if you're not quite sure you're doing the right thing.'

Relieved that Ruth hadn't noticed the way she really felt about Liam, she told her, 'I suppose I'm not, really.'

'That's only because you don't like the thought of any change in your routine. But it's going to change anyway when I leave, so it seems a good time to do it, doesn't it?'

'You're right, of course.' She grinned. 'Like you said the other day. I've become a stick-in-the-mud!'

Ruth seemed to accept her explanation and they spent the rest of the journey talking about what Ruth would need before she left for university.

'Did you eat with Lisa?' Bea asked as they arrived home.

'I did, but it was early. I'm starving again now.'

'So am I. Shall we treat ourselves and ring for a pizza?'

'I'll do it.' She consulted the list on the noticeboard. 'Hawaiian all right?'

While she was hanging up her jacket Bea's thoughts returned to Liam and what Jenny had said just before she'd left. Until that moment, Bea had thoroughly enjoyed the afternoon. She had liked the garrulous Jenny on sight, Stan, too. But, despite her reassurance to Ruth, Bea was aware that Jenny had left doubts in her mind about Liam.

Even though, and perhaps because, she had no intention of becoming involved with her itinerant house guest, she did want to know that he could be trusted. Jenny had sown doubts about that, so the moment she saw him on Monday she would press him to keep his promise.

Something that on Monday proved impossible. As Bea drove to work alone on Monday morning, she turned her car radio to the local news programme.

The item at the head of the news started, 'The man admitted to hospital last week suffering from Legionnaires' disease died last night. He was seventy-seven. Meanwhile, another patient admitted last Thursday is thought to be suffering from the disease.' The newsreader then went on to make at least two mountains out of the events.

Bea groaned. She supposed the new case they were talking about was Bert Lane. They were in for another influx of patients, especially if the media discovered he'd been admitted from their premises.

She groaned again when she saw the crowded waiting

room. She barely exchanged a word with Liam all morning unless it was concerned with work. When she went to ask him something towards the end of the morning he gave her the answer she was looking for, then raised his eyebrows and shook his head.

'It's like a menagerie today.' He smiled and patted her hand. 'The moment this madness dies down a bit, we'll go out for a meal and chat. We owe it to ourselves.'

For the remainder of that week it was all they could do to try and contain the deluge of patients and enquiries, and Bea suspected it wasn't going to be much better the next week, especially when every time she left the health centre she was harassed by members of the media, trying to glean any fragment of information from an unwary member of staff.

Bea was off duty one Saturday each month and to her relief it was the next day, but she knew Liam would be on call all weekend. She walked out to the car park late on the Friday and she was so tired that she irritably brushed off a keen junior reporter. As she reached her car, John came up behind her. 'You can't go on working hours like this, Bea. The moment the dust begins to settle we'll get down to interviewing for a part-time nurse. You will sit in and give your opinion?'

She was so exhausted from dealing with panicking patients that she nodded gratefully. Despite a weekend of doing nothing, she was still tired when she returned to work on Monday morning. She hadn't even found the energy to visit Sharon in hospital as she'd intended. As she'd suspected, it was nearly as bad a week as the previous one.

Liam was just as overwhelmed with patients and

every time she saw him he appeared increasingly exhausted.

They couldn't go on like this. Any of them. She so badly wanted to talk to Liam, but it seemed the only time they had to converse was when they discussed the patients. 'You remember the Crays?' he asked one lunchtime.

She nodded. 'Came to the smear clinic, asking about infertility treatment?'

'That's right.'

'I've got some test results back and she needs some help with her ovulation. She's starting on clomiphene pronto and if that doesn't do the trick we'll have to look further.'

'How's she feel about that?'

'Pass. He's happy we're doing something, but I'm still not sure about her.'

'It's usually the other way round, isn't it?'

'In my experience, yes. It'll be interesting to see what happens.'

They fell silent and she asked, 'Do you know when you'll be moving in?'

'If it's OK by you,' he replied, exhaustion plain on his face, 'I'll make it next weekend. Possibly Sunday. I'm second on call that day so I can hopefully do it without being disturbed too often. OK if I let you know definitely some time next week?'

'Fine.' She waited for him to suggest they get together for the chat he'd promised, but he said nothing and she guessed it was unfair of her to expect him to. He looked so totally washed-out she guessed he would probably spend the weekend sleeping.

As she made her way back to her room she remembered Ruth's comments about his noisy digs and wondered if his tiredness was made worse by lack of sleep.

She turned and, seeing him coming from his room, said diffidently, 'Would you sleep better in our spare room—small as it is?'

He shook his head. 'I'm too tired to contemplate moving anywhere at the moment—in fact, doing anything apart from rolling into bed.'

'You're welcome as a guest, Liam. You don't have to move until you're ready.'

He smiled his thanks. 'That's a very kind offer, Bea, and I appreciate it, but I'm so tired I'd sleep anywhere at the moment.'

'The offer's there if you change your mind.' Already regretting her impulsive gesture, she made a hasty exit, her cheeks stained with colour by what she saw as a pointed refusal. What must he think of her repeated impetuous offers? That she couldn't wait to get her hands on him? One thing was for sure. After that rebuff, she wouldn't make another. If there was anything at all he wanted he would have to come and ask.

When she arrived at the health centre on Monday morning, she was surprised to see John at the reception desk. 'I've had to rearrange some of your appointments. I've pushed into your list some of those booked in for Liam. If you can't deal with them, I'll see them.'

'Is Liam—?'

Before she could finish her question John answered it. 'I've told him to take the day off. It's not been an easy couple of weeks for him. I must start my list now. Don't forget. Any you're not happy to deal with, call me.'

Bea could do nothing but agree, but that didn't mean

she wasn't surprised. Liam was much younger than
John and he seemed to have survived. Between her first
few patients she puzzled over the reason for Liam's
absence, but in the end she conceded it probably *would*
have been much harder for him as he knew none of the
patients who were panicking.

When Ruth came home that night Bea asked if she'd
heard why Liam hadn't been in, but it seemed all any
of them knew was that John had told him to take the
day off.

And when he came in bright and ready for work on
Tuesday morning, she guessed she must have been
right.

CHAPTER EIGHT

WHEN she eventually rolled out of bed on Sunday, in sharp contrast to how Bea was feeling, Ruth was looking forward to Liam moving in.

'Shall I put some flowers in the room or is that sissy?'

'Whatever you like. We haven't a clue how much of his own paraphernalia he'll need room for. I'm not sure if I should clear one of the kitchen cupboards for him either. Or if he'll bring his own bedding.'

Sensing her mother's apprehension about his impending move, Ruth muttered in exasperation, 'I thought as responsible adults you'd have talked all this through. If you're doing all this, we're obviously not going to church this week, so why don't you invite him for lunch? If he's on call, he'll probably welcome it and you can find out exactly what he does need.'

'I don't know his number.'

Ruth gasped, 'Honestly, Mum. That's a feeble excuse. You of all people should know you can reach him through the emergency call service. I don't know why you're making such a big thing about having someone living here.'

Bea was about to protest when Ruth added, 'Do you want to ask him, or shall I?'

'You do it. I must get on with the cooking.' She wanted to think, undisturbed.

'What *is* the matter with you?' she rasped at herself as she bent to put the meat into the oven, aware that Ruth had touched a nerve when she'd commented that her baking had prevented their usual Sunday attendance at the morning service.

There was no reason, apart from her need to make a good impression on Liam. Surely you know him well enough by this time to know it isn't necessary, and to trust him?

But did she? Could she? He'd never enlightened her as to what Jenny had been talking about. OK, they'd had a couple of frantically busy weeks at the health centre, but had he just used that as an excuse to keep his own counsel? Why?

Ruth broke into her reverie. 'He'll be here at one, call-outs permitting. Anything I can do?'

'I—I don't think so.' Bea wanted to keep busy, and yet she needed time to think. Time to try and rationalise how she felt so that she could return to behaving reasonably again. Because she realised that since Liam's arrival on the scene she had been doing anything but. She hated the feeling that she had lost control. For nearly twenty years she had known exactly where she was going and how she was going to go about it.

She and Ruth had joked about it, but had it been her hormones that had caused this rush of blood to her head? Some women did start their menopause as early as this. Perhaps she was one of them and her body, sensing this was her last opportunity, was betraying her.

The telephone rang as the lunch was nearly ready, and she left it for Ruth to answer. Although she wasn't surprised by it, she was disappointed to think Liam was going to be late as she'd wanted the meal to be perfect.

Ruth was still talking when the doorbell rang so, cursing the interruption, she flung open the door to find Liam standing there.

She'd been so convinced that it had been Liam Ruth

was talking to on the phone that she uttered a gasp of surprise.

He raised an eyebrow and queried, 'Weren't you expecting me?'

She gulped. 'Yes…yes, come in. Do come in.'

He smiled and, closing the door behind him, leaned over and kissed her gently on the lips. 'You look beautiful.'

Conscious that she must look a fright with her cheeks flushed from the heat of the cooker, she pulled away from him.

'I—I thought you'd been delayed.'

He frowned and followed her through to the kitchen and pulled her close again. 'I'm not late, am I?'

'No— It, er, it—'

He silenced her stumbling explanation, this time with a kiss that was far from gentle and which unleashed myriad sensations Bea hadn't thought herself capable of experiencing. He only released her when Ruth clattered down the stairs.

'Good, we can eat now Liam's here.'

'Yes.' Bea struggled to return her voice to normal. 'We—we're in the kitchen.' When Ruth came in she was draining the vegetables with intense concentration.

'Anything I can do to help, Bea?'

'You can carve if you like. Ruth can take the dishes of veg through.'

'Who usually carves?' he asked, making a very competent job of removing slices from the beef joint.

'I do, but even after all these years I'm no expert.'

'Maybe not at carving, but this meat is cooked just as I like it, slightly rare. I'm going to enjoy this meal.'

He carried the plates through to the dining room, and as she followed Bea tried vainly to straighten her hair.

Once they'd all been served with veg, she asked Ruth, 'Who was it on the phone?'

'Debbie. She wants me to go over later this afternoon to meet some chaps who were helping her dad with the service this morning. She says they were fantastic.'

'Debbie's the local vicar's daughter,' Bea explained, for Liam's benefit.

He nodded.

'Who exactly are they?' Bea wanted to know.

'Simon, Peter and Co.'

Liam spluttered helplessly with laughter.

'What's so funny?' Ruth asked petulantly.

'Sorry. When you said the names I had a vision of a couple of two-thousand-year-olds.'

Bea joined in his laughter. 'The disciples. Of course.'

'They're theology students who've formed a theatre group and they call themselves that to attract attention. Those aren't their real names.' Ruth clearly resented their amusement, but whether on the group's behalf or her own, Bea wasn't sure. 'I'm sorry I missed them.'

'If they're at the church again tonight, we could go and see them.' Bea saw an opportunity to escape Liam's company on his first evening in residence.

'I've already said I'll go with Debbie, so don't expect me home until later.'

Bea nodded. 'When are you going?'

'As soon as I've helped clear away and helped Liam move in.' She didn't seem quite so enthusiastic about the latter and Bea guessed his laughter had ruffled her feelings.

He appeared to enjoy his meal, and was very enthusiastic about the apple tart Bea had made. 'You can't beat home cooking and I can see you enjoy doing it. I noticed a super cherry cake cooling in the kitchen as well.'

Afraid he would expect it every week, she warned, 'I do enjoy it, but I don't often have time for it. Ruth and I usually go to church Sunday morning.'

'But not today.' It was a statement rather than a question, and the colour that had gradually subsided from Bea's cheeks during the meal crept back across her cheeks.

'I—I overslept.' She started to clear the dishes. 'I can do this, Ruth, if you want to get off to Debbie's.'

Her daughter didn't have to be told twice.

Liam took the dishes from her. '*We* can do this, Bea. I'm not expecting you to wait on me, remember.'

Wanting to keep him at a distance, she retorted, 'I know. But you haven't moved in yet. Today is different.'

He laughed and teased, 'If you just wait for a moment, I'll collect my bags from the car and dump them in the bedroom, then I can help you do them.'

His good humour was infectious. 'You don't have to, but if you insist…'

Bea couldn't ever remember having enjoyed the washing-up so much. They chatted and laughed throughout the process, then sat down at the kitchen table with the coffee-pot between them.

'Just think what we'd have missed if you had a dishwasher.' Liam reached a hand across the table and rested it over hers.

Bea sighed, suddenly serious. 'Liam…I—'

'You don't have to ask, Bea. I know I promised to reveal all about my past, and I'm sorry not to have got round to it before this. But it's not easy to talk about, so the last thing I wanted to do was rush it, or risk being interrupted.'

She waited, not speaking but curiously searching his face.

Their eyes locked momentarily and she thought she saw a sadness there, mingled with the exhaustion which still seemed to linger.

'My father died when I was relatively young and, like Ruth, I was brought up by my mother on her own. When she died it was a couple of months before my sixteenth birthday. Too old for a children's home, but the authorities considered me too young to take over the tenancy of Mum's council-owned house.'

His hand was still resting over hers and she felt it tense as he spoke.

'I'd met Jenny and Stan through their daughter, Deanna, who was in my class at school. They heard about my plight and offered me a home.'

Bea nodded but, not wanting to break his mood, she still didn't speak.

'As you saw for yourself, they are kindness personified, and they treated me like a son. Especially when Deanna and I started to date.'

'Yes?' Bea prompted when he hesitated, clearly affected by his memories.

'We were working for our A-levels, and as I wanted good grades to get to medical school, I refused to go with her to a gig in Chester. She went with a group of girls and met...' He took a deep breath, continuing, 'She met a drop-out who was a drug addict.'

'Oh, Liam!' Bea breathed.

'She thought him much more interesting than a bookworm like me, and she neglected her studies to go out with him almost every night.

'When she realised she didn't stand a chance of getting even one A-level, she told her parents she loved him and went off to live with him.'

'How awful for them.'

He nodded. 'It was, and is.' He paused as if he needed time to pull himself together. 'There was a lot of acrimony at the time and, though he died several years ago, she has consistently refused to have anything to do with them.'

'Lucky they had you,' she said softly.

'I'm not so sure about that. If they hadn't taken me in, perhaps it would never have happened. I did try several times to reason with her, but she accused me of being jealous and I could see I was making matters worse so I took myself off to medical school and hoped she might move back.'

'She didn't?'

'No. And it left me unsure what to do. I felt it wasn't fair to hurt Stan and Jenny again by cutting myself right off from them, but I do wonder if my continued contact is keeping her away. But when I try to discuss it with them, they beg me to keep visiting. That's why I decided to go abroad.'

'Is she on drugs?'

'Not as far as I know. She's actually holding down quite a responsible job.'

Recalling his bitter remark about girls like Cilla thinking bad characters more attractive, she asked, 'Did—do you still care about her?'

He gave her a long and penetrating look before answering. 'I was seventeen, Bea. We'd been thrown together. She was good company. I don't think I am, or ever was, ''in love'' with her, if that's what you mean, but for Stan's and Jenny's sakes I still care about her.'

Bea was silent, sensing the hurt and hopelessness he was experiencing.

'I'm not finding telling you this easy. It's something I never speak about because I feel it would be disloyal to the two people who have been so good to me. But Jenny having said what she did, I knew I'd have to make the effort, but I kept putting it off, pretending to myself I needed time to do it properly. Time which work hasn't allowed recently.'

'I understand, Liam.' Bea grasped his now clenched hand between both of hers and he added his other hand to the clasp, pulling her gently towards him so that he could look closely into her eyes.

'I believe you do, Bea. I believe you do.' He raised their clasped hands to his cheek and she felt moisture there. 'You don't know how good it is to have shared this with someone. Someone not involved, that is.'

She smiled and said softly, 'Talking through our problems is good for us all, Liam. Now you've made a start, I'll be here to listen at any time.'

'You're a pretty special person, Beatrice Seton. I knew that the moment I set eyes on you.'

He leaned across the table and, placing their clasped hands over his heart, kissed her firmly on the lips, then nibbled them gently as he murmured, 'You beat after-dinner mints hollow.'

When the pressure of the table between them finally became too uncomfortable, he reluctantly released her.

She smiled up at him, her eyes misty. 'I only promised to listen to you, Liam. I don't think you should take advantage of your landlady like this.'

'We had a chaperone.' He indicated the table. 'But I think we'll dispense with its services.' He moved around it towards her.

Realising he was encouraged by her unconscious response, she started to back away. 'I don't think this is a good idea, Liam.' He might enjoy flirting with her, even enticing her into his bed, but she had to remember that in less than five months he would be gone.

She was older and wiser than she had been as a teenager, and she knew any such involvement would result in pain and heartbreak.

He had returned to his seat and was watching her quizzically as she struggled with her thoughts.

'Why?' he asked her softly.

'Why?' To hide her confusion she pretended not to understand.

'Why is it not a good idea?'

'Because we have to work together, because we'll be living under the same roof and because of Ruth and...' She searched unsuccessfully for more reasons that wouldn't reveal the truth which was insistently pulsing through her brain. That she was too vulnerable to handle her dangerous attraction to him.

'And you still don't trust me?' he wryly supplied for her.

She flopped down on the dining-room chair farthest away from him and seized the opportunity to escape the rising tension of their exchange. 'I've offered you a room, haven't I?' She ignored his look of disbelief and continued, 'And that being the case, I think it would be a good idea if I give you a front-door key and we get you moved you in now. Just in case you're called out and the house is empty when you return.'

He shook his head and raised himself from his seat so slowly that his reluctance was obvious, but Bea was determined. She pulled open one of the kitchen drawers and took out two keys on a ring. 'This one is for the porch door, and this for the front door. Would you like me to provide a lock on your bedroom door as well?'

He took the keys with an ironic smile. 'Unfortunately, I see no prospect of it being necessary. But what about you? Would you be happier if I was locked in?'

She flushed at his sarcasm and, ignoring it, asked, 'Can I help carry anything in?'

'I can manage, thanks.' He made his way out to his car and Bea uttered a sigh of relief. If she could just keep this verbal barrier between them it would work. It was only for five months after all.

Today had been a lesson for her. She mustn't relax her guard for a moment and allow such a situation to arise again. Ruth would be there to start with and that should diffuse any tension between them, but if Ruth did happen to be out when he was in the house, she knew now what could happen, and had to take steps to prevent it.

She followed him to the door and he handed her a small overnight bag. 'I'll bring the rest.'

She quickly carried the bag up the stairs and left it on the floor beside his bed.

He carried a case and a heavy bag up to his room, then went back for a small box of books. Finally he locked the car and, closing the front door behind him, brought a box of oddments through to the kitchen.

'You might have a use for some of these gadgets. There are a couple of tins as well and some cereal. Do you want to add it to your store cupboard?'

'As you like.' She listed a quick inventory of the contents of each of her kitchen cupboards.

'Are you unpacking before you go back for the rest?'

'What rest? I told you, I travel light.'

To hide her embarrassment at her mistake, she turned

to refill the water filtering jug, and to her dismay felt tears of pity pricking at the back of her eyes. She was experiencing a deep sadness for the circumstances that had made him reach a similar age to herself with little love in his life and few possessions to call his own.

He must have sensed her thoughts because he said quietly, 'I am going abroad, don't forget. I won't need much in Malaysia.'

How could she forget? If he hadn't been going abroad things might have been very different, but there was no future for any kind of a relationship under the circumstances.

And there was no guarantee there would have been if they were different! He hadn't exactly put his feelings on the line, only toyed with her affection. If he hadn't known it would be limited by him moving on, would he feel the same? And what about her? She had been attracted to him from the first day they'd met, but was it more than that, or was it pity for the rotten deal he'd received in life that was now tearing at her heart?

Whichever, she couldn't keep filling the filter reservoir with water! She turned and smiled. 'We all tend to be a bit too attached to our worldly goods, don't we?'

'Things were different for you. You needed to make a home for your daughter.'

'I suppose you're right.' She yawned, overtaken by a surge of emotional and post-prandial exhaustion, no doubt fuelled by her lack of sleep the previous night.

'I'm going into the garden for a breath of fresh air,' she told him. 'The weeds are creeping up on me again.'

'Can I help?'

'What about your unpacking?'

'All in good time.' He followed her into the diminutive back garden.

'It's not up to Jenny's standard, I'm afraid.'

'That wouldn't be easy in a patch this size, and don't forget Jenny is at home all day.'

He stood back and surveyed the whole effect. 'I like the shrubs—especially the way you've varied the leaf colours.'

She had planted them to give some privacy from the neighbours. 'I asked at the garden centre for varieties that don't grow much above five feet, but if I didn't keep cutting them back I'd have a forest!'

He laughed. 'Jenny had a fir tree that was given to her as a bonsai plant. She didn't cut it back and it reverted to grow to well over eleven feet! She was very annoyed about that.'

'I can imagine.'

'I can't see that many weeds, but I'll remove those that there are from this side if you like.'

She nodded and brought a trug from the garage, together with small shears to trim the edge of the tiny patch of grass that was home to the rotary washing line.

After toiling in the warm sun for some time, she stood to straighten her back for a moment and cannoned into Liam's bent back.

Swinging round, he caught her off balance and steadied her.

'I warned you there wasn't room for two out here.' She laughed, putting her hands out defensively.

Taking a firm grasp on her arms, he joined in her laughter. 'And I told you it might be fun. And it is!' He leaned forward and dropped a light kiss on her nose.

'Liam, someone might be watching!'

'What if they are? We're both free agents.'

'I know, but… I'm going to find a cold drink. Would

you like one?' She wanted to escape. 'There's lemon squash or Coke or—'

'Lemon would be fine.'

By the time she returned with the drinks, the garden was neat and tidy and he had disposed of the weeds into the wheelie bin and put away the shears.

They sat side by side on the tiny wooden bench her father and mother had given her for her birthday the previous year.

Neither of them spoke, and when Bea turned to look at him she saw that his eyes were closed and his face lifted up to the sun.

Her eyes searched his face compassionately.

Their peace was shattered by the strident tone of Liam's bleeper. He checked the number and with a rueful smile set off indoors. 'I left my mobile in the kitchen.'

'Use the one in the dining room if you like.' She followed him into the house and put their empty glasses in the sink.

When he'd finished talking, he came in search of her. 'I have to go. Feverish child and fretful mother who's convinced he has meningitis. Alicia is with a suspected heart attack.'

'Would you like me to come?'

She thought he was about to refuse, but then he said, 'It might be a good idea. You probably know a lot more about babies than I do.'

As they drove across the town, she asked, 'How old?'

'The baby? Seventeen months, I think she said.'

'What's his name? I probably know him.'

He shook his head. 'They're from Birmingham. Just visiting. Gran's on our books. Mrs Malone, I think she said.'

'I know her well. She's a dreadful worrier and has an out-of-date book of family medicine that she always reads up so that she can make her own diagnosis. Trouble is, she's usually wrong and refuses to believe the correct one if it's less serious.'

'In other words, she enjoys bad health. If daughter's anything like mother this isn't going to be easy, is it?'

'You *could* say that. Perhaps our saving grace will be that she hasn't a daughter, only a son.'

'What's he like?'

'I haven't met him.'

When Liam drew the car to a halt outside the address he'd been given, Bea groaned.

'What's the matter?'

'Looks like the baby's father jumping up and down on the doorstep.'

'Hmm. He *is* agitated, isn't he? Come on, let's get it over with.'

Liam lifted his bag from the car and they made their way into the house.

'It's meningitis, Doctor.' Mrs Malone nodded towards Liam. 'He *is* a doctor, isn't he?'

'A very good one,' Bea told her reassuringly, 'especially with children.' She lifted the toddler from her arms. 'Let's have a look at him. What's he called?'

'Sean.'

Despite the warmth of the day, the toddler was dressed in layers of woollen coats and wrapped in a blanket. His cheeks were a fiery red.

'I don't think he needs all this today,' Bea told his mother gently.

'But—but Del's mum says as he's feverish. I have to wrap him up.'

'Have you checked his temperature?' Liam asked.

Mrs Malone broke in on the conversation. 'Don't need to. Them fiery cheeks are a dead give-away.'

Bea removed the jumper the now unwrapped child was wearing.

He watched her every movement with wide eyes, but though he'd been whimpering pitifully when they'd come in he soon stopped.

'He's got a rash on his arm,' Mrs Malone announced triumphantly. 'He should be in hospital.'

Liam didn't answer. With Bea's help he was examining the child thoroughly. Sean took a great interest in everything he was doing and didn't appear to object to any of the range of movements Liam subjected him to.

'Has he been in contact with older children?' Liam asked his mother.

She nodded. 'His childminder has two children at infant school. He's with them every afternoon after school.'

'I thought as much. Sean is suffering from slapped cheek disease.'

'What's that?' his mother asked.

'What about his rash?' Mrs Malone blustered. 'You're not telling us the truth. It's meningitis. I know it is.'

'Mrs Malone,' Liam told her firmly, 'your grandson does not have meningitis.' He pressed his finger over some of the spots. 'The spots in meningitis are quite different.'

'Does he need treatment?' Sean's mother was panicking.

'Just tender loving care.'

When Mrs Malone started to object, Liam took Sean from Bea's arms and motioned for his mother and father to follow him into the kitchen.

Bea met his eyes and he indicated with a movement of his head what he wanted her to do. She quickly closed the door behind them and, taking hold of Mrs Malone, seated her gently.

'You're upsetting your son and daughter-in-law. Sean's fine. That's a kind of rash on his cheeks, not an indication that he's feverish.'

Mrs Malone's face crumpled and, as Bea watched, her belligerent attitude was replaced by a noisy sobbing.

Bea drew up a chair beside her and put an arm around her shoulder.

The older woman eventually lifted her tear-stained face to look at Bea. 'But he was so miserable.'

'He was too warm in all that clothing and he could sense your anxiety. Children do, you know, and it affects them more than you'd believe possible. As you saw, he was fine while we were taking a look at him. It's nothing to worry about at all.'

Mrs Malone started sobbing afresh. 'You're sure?'

'Dr Taylor is sure, and that's enough for me,' Bea said quietly.

'Thank you, Nurse. Thank you. You don't know what a relief it is to hear that.' She scrubbed at her face with a tissue and tried to smile. 'I'm sorry to make such a fuss.'

'We'd rather you called us when you're worried like this than ignored something serious.'

'My daughter died of meningitis.' The statement was uttered in a flat monotone that made Bea shiver despite the warmth of the day.

'I'm sorry. I'd no idea.'

Mrs Malone nodded wearily. 'It was a long time ago. I didn't call the doctor. I've never forgiven myself.'

Bea hugged the older woman to her. 'You mustn't

blame yourself—it wasn't your fault. It's only in recent years that publicity has made us aware of the symptoms to look for.'

'You're right, of course. But it doesn't make it any easier. Especially as I couldn't have any more children.'

'You already had your son?'

She nodded. 'He was two years older.'

'And now he's produced a super grandchild for you to love.'

Mrs Malone smiled for the first time as Liam came back into the room with Sean and his mother.

Liam flashed Bea a look of amazement as Mrs Malone offered them a cup of tea.

'No, thanks, we must get on today.' He led the way to the front door and Bea followed.

'Thank you very much, Doctor. And you, Nurse.'

Once they were on their way back to Bea's house, Liam rested a hand on her knee and said, 'I don't know how you did it, but thanks a million.'

'Mmm.' Bea was deep in thought. 'Poor woman. What she must have put herself through over the years.'

Liam frowned as he replaced his hand on the steering-wheel. 'Mrs Malone, you mean?'

Bea nodded. 'All the things I've thought and said about her. I feel awful.'

'I don't understand.'

Bea shook her head sadly. 'She lost her daughter to meningitis. She's been blaming herself ever since for not calling the doctor. No wonder she consults that book now and panics.'

'What did you say to her?'

'What could I say, except the obvious? That at that time there wasn't the publicity about the symptoms.'

His hand returned to her knee in a gesture of sympathy that released some of the tears pricking behind her eyes.

He pulled the car to a stop and the moment they were inside the door he pulled her into his arms. 'You old softie…' He kissed her eyelids and wiped the tears from her cheek with his thumb. 'You really care, don't you?'

'I can't help thinking how *I'd* have felt if it had been Ruth. I'd never forgive myself either.' Overwrought, she released herself from his hold and wiped a stray tear from her eye. 'It makes me realise the importance of health education. I'll put a much greater stress on it in the future.'

'We do already, love.' Liam had hoped to make her forget work for the time being, but she was so fired up with remorse that she didn't even notice he'd spoken.

'We strew the waiting room with leaflets and posters, but how many of our patients bother to look at them? There's an information overload out there. I bet if you asked them if they've found any of the information of interest, the answer wouldn't only be just no—it would be, "What information?" There's just too much out there to sift through.'

'Yes, but—'

'I've always believed health education needs to be done on a one-to-one basis and I'm right, aren't I?' Bea didn't wait for his reply. 'Pressure of work has made me neglect it recently. Thank goodness John has agreed to another pair of hands. Once I have help I can make it my number-one priority.'

His emotions stirred by her reaction to the situation, Liam wanted to tell her so, to show her how much he loved the way she cared so much about the patients. But he recognised that for the moment she needed to do something practical, or at least make plans to do so.

She wouldn't even listen until she felt she could make a difference, and there was no point in him trying to talk about anything else until the unnecessary guilt she was feeling began to subside.

CHAPTER NINE

LIAM moved through to the kitchen and made a pot of tea. When he brought it through to the living room in a couple of china mugs, Bea covered her face with her hands and groaned. 'I'm sorry, Liam. I've been a bore, haven't I? Once I sense something wrong, I can't rest until I put it right. I still feel dreadful about Mrs Malone. It's so easy to mock rather than look for the reason behind someone's behaviour.'

'After working with you for the last month, I should think you are the least guilty of that of all of us. If anything, you care about people too much and take their problems home with you.' He smiled and teased, 'But I found your sackcloth and ashes very attractive. You've no idea how beautiful you are when aroused. It took every ounce of my will-power not to drag you upstairs and make mad, passionate love to you to give you something else to think about.'

Her wide eyes looked like those of a startled fawn when she looked up at him, and he rushed to reassure her with a laugh. 'But as it's my first day under your roof, I thought it best not to.'

When he saw she was still uneasy, he settled in the chair opposite her and said gently, 'It was a compliment, Bea. Nothing more, nothing less.' When she still didn't relax, he realised just how deeply she'd been traumatised by her earlier mistake and said, 'I chose an unfortunate way of putting it, Bea, and I apologise. I don't want you to feel you need to put a lock on your bedroom door.'

She sipped her tea and rewarded him with a smile, a little wan maybe but it was a smile at least. 'I shouldn't have reacted the way I did, but having someone else in the house is very new to me and I'm not finding it easy.'

'I understand and I'll give you plenty of space and time to yourself, Bea. That's what you're most afraid of losing, isn't it? In fact, I'll make a start by getting on with my unpacking now and giving you your Sunday afternoon back.'

'I certainly don't expect you to stay cooped up in your bedroom.'

'I'm relieved to hear it.' He started towards the door.

'And, Liam?' He turned back to her hopefully. 'Thanks for the tea. I certainly don't object to being waited on for a change.'

He made his way to his room with a wry smile. What on earth had possessed him to go in with all guns blazing the way he had? Before he'd moved in he'd recognised her hang-ups about a relationship, and had intended to take things very slowly, but she had been so upset by their visit to Mrs Malone that he'd wanted to cheer her up. He'd achieved the exact opposite and had probably destroyed what little trust she already had in him.

Bea remained seated, gazing longingly at the door Liam had closed behind him. She should never have invited him into her home. She was far too attracted to him.

As he'd hinted, once Ruth had left for university she would need space to find her new role in life and, however much she might be tempted, it wouldn't include a transient affair with Liam. Or anyone else.

Not that anyone else had ever awoken the feelings in her that Liam had, and at this moment she doubted if they ever would. Because she'd definitely fallen in love with him—she couldn't deny it—but it was dangerous in the extreme when they were living under the same roof. Especially when he didn't appear to feel as she did. Oh, he was obviously attracted to her, but if it was something more he'd have said so by now and he hadn't.

Apart from the opening and shutting of drawers, the house was so quiet that she heard his mobile phone ring. So she wasn't surprised when he came downstairs and told her, 'Another call. Sounds like an ectopic pregnancy. See you some time.'

'Would you like me to come?' she offered tentatively.

'No way,' he answered vehemently. 'You need your time off.' He slammed the front door behind him.

She sat in the silence, stunned by his rebuff. He'd not thought about her time off when they'd visited the toddler so what was different this time?

She shrugged. It could only be that he was regretting what had happened on their return and wanted to avoid a repetition.

The house seemed quiet without Ruth as well, and Bea decided to go to the evening service and see the youngsters Debbie had been so enthusiastic about.

She enjoyed the service. It was lively and warm and she felt much calmer about things as she returned home. Liam still wasn't back, so she presumed he'd been called out again. As they'd had a cooked lunch, she decided against making an evening meal for any of them and contented herself with a sandwich.

Ruth was the first back, bouncing in around ten. 'Enjoy yourself?' Bea asked.

'It was great, wasn't it? Did you like Ben and Dave's part of the service?' She was so full of enthusiasm that she didn't wait for Bea's answer. 'We thought they were terrific. Hope they don't become stuffy once they're ordained.'

Bea laughed. 'Are you implying Debbie's dad is stuffy?'

'Nah, but you know what I mean.'

'Yes, I know. And I did enjoy it. Do you want anything to eat?'

'No. We all went for a burger. How's Liam settled in?'

Bea tried unsuccessfully to fight the eruption of colour in her cheeks. 'He hasn't really had much chance. I went with him on one visit and after we'd had a cup of tea he was called out again. I haven't seen him since.'

'Must have been some cup of tea to make you blush the way you are, Mum.'

Bea cursed her easy relationship with Ruth which allowed her to make comments like that. 'Sorry to disappoint you but that's all it was.'

The sound of a key in the front door prevented Ruth replying. Looking absolutely exhausted, Liam joined them.

'Difficult evening?' Bea asked.

He nodded. 'Lost two, saved one.'

Ruth gasped and Bea jumped to her feet. 'Can I get you something to eat?'

He pushed her gently back into her seat and smiled. 'I don't expect you to wait on me. I'll get myself a coffee. That's all I want.'

Ruth offered. 'I'll get it. I'd like one myself.'

She rushed out to the kitchen and Liam yawned and perched on the edge of an upright chair. 'Make yourself comfortable.' Bea indicated the empty easy chair.

He shook his head. 'I'll be asleep if I do that. I'll take my coffee up and make a space so that I can get to bed.'

Bea guessed he couldn't have had time to do much unpacking, and asked, 'Anything I can do to help?'

He shook his head. 'I'll be fine.'

Bea guessed by the way he avoided her gaze that he was remembering her earlier reaction. Wondering if she'd also forfeited the right to be his confidante, she murmured, 'Would it help to talk about what happened on your visits?'

He shook his head and said, 'I just need sleep in case I'm called again.'

He took the mug of coffee Ruth brought at that moment, wished them both goodnight and left.

Ruth kicked the door closed behind him. 'What have you done, Mum? Told him the lodger's place is in his bedroom?'

'Of course not, silly.'

Ruth's sideways looked told Bea she didn't believe her, which wasn't surprising as Bea herself was already wondering if Liam thought that was what she'd implied.

'I'm off to bed as well.'

'You never go this early.'

Bea silently cursed her daughter's perception and snapped, 'Well, I'm tired tonight.'

She found it hard to settle, knowing Liam was in the next room, but eventually she slept. As far she knew, he wasn't called out again, and when she came down for breakfast he had already had his.

'Hope you don't mind, but I want an early start.'

'You don't have to make excuses. This is your home now. I'll see you later at the health centre.'

She did see him, but not to talk to, and whenever he did have a free moment someone else always managed to buttonhole him first.

The week passed without them conversing about anything meaningful, yet she had to admit Liam had fitted well into the household. If he was in first, he prepared the meal for them all, and if either she or Ruth did the cooking, he always undertook the clearing-away and washing-up.

Unless he was called out, once he'd retired to his room he never emerged until rising to use the bathroom before either of them needed it, and if he didn't have an early start at work, he visited the gym he belonged to.

On Thursday night he told her he was going up to visit Jenny and Stan for the weekend, and asked her to show him how to use the washing machine.

'You don't *have* to do it yourself. I understand if you'd prefer to, but I don't mind putting it in with ours. And, of course, I'll do the towels and bedding.'

'I've rather a lot, with going to the gym.'

Reading his questioning tone as meaning he wouldn't object if she insisted on doing it, she told him, 'It's up to you.'

'Well, if you're sure. Especially as I'm away this weekend.'

On Saturday afternoon, Bea was loading the washing machine when Ruth said, 'I'm off to the shops now, Mum. What would you like for your birthday?'

'My birthday? Bea checked the calendar. 'Gosh, it's on Friday, isn't it? Where does the time go? I'm getting far too old to think about such things.'

Ruth teased, 'You always say that and you know you don't mean it.'

'I do this year. Anyway, I don't want you spending a lot on me because you're going to need all your earnings and more when you get to university.'

'I know that, Mum, but a present won't break me.'

'You'll have to choose it yourself, then. I haven't a clue.'

'You're hopeless! See you later.'

Bea continued to lift the dirty washing from the laundry basket and she paused with the shirt Liam had worn the day before in her hand. The scent of him still clinging to the fabric evoked a strong memory of being in his arms on their return from the visit to Mrs Malone.

She brought it closer to her face and a sudden longing for him overwhelmed her. She was tempted, so tempted at that moment to throw caution to the winds on his return, but she knew that if she did, when the time came for him to leave she would regret it.

She thrust the garment into the machine and started the programme, hoping to wash away her fantasies about him.

But it wasn't quite as easy as that. Ruth rang to say she was going on to Debbie's house for the evening, and Bea suddenly had far too much time on her hands not to think about how much she missed having Liam about the house already.

It was a relief when Sunday came and Ruth was there to take her mind off her thoughts. They followed their usual routine—morning service followed by a roast lunch.

For once Bea was thankful for her daughter's constant chatter over the meal and the sound of her music when she went to her room to start sorting out what she thought she might take to university.

Wanting to make the most of the two weeks until Ruth left, Bea went up to see if she could help. They had a riotous time selecting and discarding items from Ruth's wardrobe, but it still didn't prevent insistent thoughts of Liam recurring—so much so that by the time Ruth and Debbie went out in the evening, Bea couldn't wait for his return.

She tried to tell herself it was because she wanted to hear if there was any news of Jenny's and Stan's daughter, but in reality she knew she was fooling herself.

So she was more than disappointed when he rang to say he would come back early the next morning and go straight to work.

'Is everything OK?' she asked him anxiously.

'Fine. And with you?'

'Ruth and I have had a great weekend, thanks. Remember me to Jenny and Stan, won't you?'

'Sure. They said not to forget to bring you up some time next month.'

'I'll look forward to it.'

She replaced the receiver, resigned to another evening with only her thoughts for company. Aware that she'd never felt so unsettled before, she told herself to snap out of it and find something to keep her occupied, but she knew that whatever she did it wouldn't prevent thoughts of Liam intruding.

He came in search of her at lunchtime on Monday. 'Do you remember Mr Gray? Had the stroke in your room? Apparently, he was discharged on Friday.'

'If you remember, I met his wife in the hospital car park one evening.'

'That's why when Alicia asked me to do a home visit

I wondered if you'd like to come along and see what you think while I assess the situation.'

She checked her diary. 'I'm free until two-thirty. Is that any good?'

'Fine. Ten minutes OK?'

She nodded. 'I'll be ready.'

As they drove to the house, Bea asked him about his weekend.

'Difficult. Sunday was Deanna's birthday. They live in hope that their card will prompt her into contacting them. As usual, it hasn't. So far, at least.'

'That's sad,' Bea breathed, thinking about her own birthday on the coming Friday and how she'd agreed to a celebratory tea with her own parents on Sunday.

'I wish there was something I could do to help but, as I said, I think I just make matters worse.'

Bea nodded. 'I know exactly what you mean. Once there's been bad feeling between close relatives it's not easy for either side to forget.'

'Sorry, Bea. You're the last person I should be saying this to, but you persevered and eventually won through.'

'I don't know. Perhaps, as I've been through something similar, I have a better understanding.'

'I'm sure you do, but you don't need to be reminded of it.'

'Forget it. We all have our problems, Liam.'

He nodded, then a few moments later he said, 'By the way, I rang the hospital again this morning. Old Bert Lane is doing well now. Your prompt action meant he started treatment early and even his diabetes is stabilising.'

'Great. Did they ever find the source?'

'No, and I doubt if they ever will if there are no more cases.'

'Let's hope there aren't. I wouldn't want to face another couple of weeks like that for a long time.'

He laughed. 'No doubt the media will come up with something else to cause us problems!'

As he finished speaking he pulled up at the green door, and Bea could see Mrs Gray at the window. She opened the door before they reached it and Bea could see that she was in a distraught state. 'I thought you said it would be different this time. He can't do any more for himself than his dad did.'

As Liam closed the front door behind them, Bea rested a soothing hand on her shoulder. 'Where is your husband?'

Mrs Gray indicated the door to the front room.

'Come through to the kitchen and tell me all about it while Dr Taylor takes a look at him.'

Liam nodded approvingly at her suggestion and knocked gently on the door, before opening it and calling, 'Mr Gray? It's Dr Taylor.'

He closed the door behind him and Mrs Gray burst into tears.

Bea guided her through to the kitchen, sat her down and, after handing her a tissue, filled the kettle with water and switched it on. Then she drew up the other chair and grasped Mrs Gray's hands in her own. When her sobbing eventually began to subside, Bea said, 'Tell me how you're coping.'

'I'm not.' She sniffed. 'He can't do anything without help and he's so miserable. The hospital said they needed his bed and that he could just as easily be rehabilitated from home, but it's going to be just like his father. He'll just sit there and nothing'll be done and I'll…' She was so upset she couldn't finish the sentence.

'All these arrangements take time. Nothing would

have been done at the weekend in hospital either. Dr Taylor will soon get you husband assessed and initiate all the services he needs if the hospital hasn't already organised it.' The kettle clicked off, and Bea made a pot of tea and lifted three mugs off the stand. 'Will Mr Gray have some tea?'

Mrs Gray nodded and sniffed, dabbing the tissue to her eyes.

'In a mug?'

Another tearful nod.

If he could manage a mug that was one good sign, Bea thought with relief as she lifted down a fourth one.

She poured the tea, and when she heard the door to the front room opening she called out cheerfully, 'Tea's ready.'

When Liam came through, she picked up two of the mugs and said, 'I'll see Mr Gray gets this.'

Liam flashed her an appreciative smile.

Bea found Mr Gray seated in a high-backed armchair. He looked very comfortable and well cared for, and smiled a lopsided greeting.

'You look much better than when I last saw you in the surgery,' Bea told him.

He nodded and with a struggle managed to say, 'I feel it.'

'I've brought you some tea,' she told him. While she helped him by steadying the mug, she looked around the room and was surprised by all the necessary aids to disabled living being there already. Mrs Gray hadn't been left without any help.

They had finished drinking their tea when Liam and Mrs Gray came back into the room.

Liam smiled. 'I've told your wife how well I think you're doing. I've organised a physio to call later in the day. I'm still trying to reach the speech therapist, but as long as you keep making the effort your speech should certainly improve. *We* can all understand what you're saying already. I'll let you know as soon as I've arranged something.' He smiled at them both.

'If there's nothing else at the moment, I'll call again tomorrow and see how it's working out.' He turned to Mrs Gray. 'If you need me in the meantime, don't hesitate to call the surgery. You've got the number?'

'I have that,' she responded fervently. 'It's on the wall by the telephone.'

When they were on the way back to the health centre, Bea exclaimed, 'She seemed to think nothing's being done, but I couldn't believe all the equipment she has in place already. They must have needed the bed pretty desperately to get all that organised so quickly.'

Liam laughed. 'You forget she's already nursed his father for many years. She tells me most of the stuff in there is their own. Apparently, the occupational therapist came on Friday morning to see what was needed, and when she saw it all there they shipped him out pronto.

'He was delighted, but as Mrs G. wasn't expecting him it came as a bit of a shock. She just needed to get it all off her chest and be assured the physio would be calling. I think we'll find she'll be OK now.'

'I see.'

He pulled up at the traffic lights, and when he'd negotiated the right turn he said, 'He's actually doing quite well, and with some intensive physio should be able to get about on his own before too long. But I will keep an eye on things. If there's any backsliding, his wife will soon be back down in the dumps.'

She nodded. 'She said *he* was depressed, but I didn't see much sign of it.'

'I think that was just part of her cry for help.'

They arrived back at the health centre in time for Bea's first afternoon appointment, and she saw nothing more of Liam until he came back to the house after evening surgery. Ruth was with him as she had been working late, and they were chattering as if they'd known one another all their lives.

Again the thought struck Bea that at this rate Ruth was going to be more devastated than she herself when Liam left. It was just as well she was soon off to university when hopefully this father-daughter-like relationship would end.

Bea was puzzled when her daughter wasn't anywhere to be found when she was ready to leave work on Tuesday evening.

'I thought Ruth'd want a lift home,' she told Katy.

The receptionist shrugged. 'She asked for a couple of hours off. Said she'll make it up when we need some extra time from her.'

Liam had also left, so Bea drove home in anticipation of there being a meal ready for her. But the house was empty.

Ruth was the first to arrive home, saying she'd been into town to get a few last-minute bits and pieces for university, and Bea was disappointed when she didn't show her what she had in the bags she was carrying.

Bea was still preoccupied when Liam arrived back just as she served the meal.

'Problems at the health centre this afternoon?' he asked with a frown.

'Not that I know of. Why? Were you out on calls?'

'Yes. Well, not exactly house calls, but there was someone I had to see.' He didn't elaborate and Bea lapsed into silence while he and Ruth conducted a light and amusing conversation about nothing in particular.

As they seemed to do every spare moment Liam had.

On Thursday afternoon, Mr Darby came in for a final check on his burn and he mentioned having seen Dr Taylor at the hospital on Tuesday. Bea was puzzled as to why Liam hadn't said that was where he had been.

Ruth was up surprisingly early on Friday morning and Bea came down to find her breakfast ready and parcels and cards on the table. 'Happy birthday, Mum.' Ruth gave her a big kiss and handed her a bulky package.

Bea opened it to find two of the latest bestsellers and two CDs by groups that were favourites of hers.

'Thank you, darling. I shall certainly enjoy all of these.'

'I thought you needed something to fill your time once I'm out of your hair!'

Liam came in and wished her many happy returns. He, too, leaned over and kissed her and handed over a parcel.

Bea gasped when she opened it and saw an exquisite antique necklace nestling in a delicate padded box. 'It's beautiful, Liam. But you shouldn't have—'

She was about to say 'spent this kind of money', but he broke in, 'Why shouldn't I spoil my landlady?'

'But this—'

'Is something to remember your first tenant by.' He grinned and checked his watch. 'I've got to go now, but Ruth tells me she's doing the cooking tonight and I'm invited. I'm looking forward to it. It's a long time since I've been to a birthday party.'

His remark about the birthday party reminded her that he had no real family, and when she and Ruth arrived at work she realised just how lucky she was. She was greeted by a chorus of birthday wishes. Liam must have been busy telling everyone, she concluded. She treated everyone to cream cakes at lunchtime and had a thoroughly enjoyable day.

Liam's list of patients on Friday evening was short, Bea discovered when she went to check if Ruth wanted a lift home. 'I'll be a little while yet, Mum, so I expect Liam will give me a lift. You go on, but leave the meal. I've got it all sorted. You just pamper yourself for once.'

She decided to do just that and was relaxing in the bath when the phone rang. She picked up the receiver to hear Ruth's voice. 'I won't be home until eightish. Liam's been called out on an emergency, so I'm getting the bus home. Rather than cook, I've booked us to eat somewhere very special, so put on your best outfit and make yourself look beautiful.'

'Where?' Bea asked.

'You wouldn't know it. Katy's just recommended it. See you.'

'Will Liam come with us?' she asked, remembering his comment about birthday parties.

'I doubt if he'll be back in time.'

Bea felt a stab of disappointment. Perversely, after keeping him at arm's length, she now wanted him to share her birthday meal. 'I could come and collect you,' she offered, thinking he could join them later if they were eating at home.

'No need for that, Mum. I'm leaving now.'

Bea climbed out of the bath, wondering what kind of an emergency could be taking Liam so long. She shrugged and made up her mind to enjoy herself anyway. She would wear that absurdly expensive silk dress and jacket she'd splashed out on the night she'd been feeling sorry for herself. It would show off the present from Liam beautifully and at least he would see how much she appreciated it when they eventually arrived home.

Her disappointment lent an edge to her voice when Ruth rushed in. 'Is Liam still not back?'

Ruth shook her head. 'You look ace. That dress is the goods and no doubt. And that necklace—wow, Mum. Liam must think you very special.'

Hot colour stained Bea's cheeks and she tried to play down the gift. 'I guess he's just so pleased to be part of a family celebration that he's gone over the top. I didn't even know he knew it was my birthday. You shouldn't have told him.'

It was Ruth's turn to blush. 'I had to tell him as I thought he'd be here for our meal tonight. Anyway, the table's booked for nine, so I'd better go and change.'

'I'll drive,' she said a few minutes later as she rejoined Bea, 'then you can have a drink to celebrate.'

'Shall we leave a note for Liam to say where we are?' Bea asked, hopeful that he might still join them.

Ruth shook her head. 'No point. He says he'll be tied up all evening. Anyway, I know what you're up to,' she told Bea with a giggle.

Surely she hadn't made her disappointment so obvious. 'I'm not up to anything,' she protested.

'You are. You're trying to find out where we're going.'

Thank goodness. If that was all Ruth suspected her of, she'd go along with it.

Ruth drove right out of Bargate and down to the next

junction on the motorway. Bea was puzzled, then shocked as Ruth pulled the car through the stone gate-posts of an old manor house and drove up the long drive to the front door with a flourish. Coloured lights twinkled from the trees that flanked the entrance.

'You can't afford a place like this,' Bea whispered.

'Don't argue,' Ruth ordered. 'It's a thank you for all you've done for me.'

Bea looked at the cars parked neatly in a line and looked again—this time more closely. She thought she'd seen Liam's car, and was peering at the number plate when the passenger door opened and a voice she knew well enquired, 'Can I escort you indoors, madam?'

Liam helped her from the car and Bea shook her head. 'How—? I thought you were detained on an urgent call.'

'I was, but she's in hospital undergoing surgery now. And am I glad. I would hate to have missed this incredible vision.' He took her arm and she could smell the faint aroma of his aftershave. 'Happy birthday again, Bea. As I thought, that's the right necklace for that outfit.'

'How did you know about it?'

'Ruth told me what you'd been up to that day you refused to eat with us on the pretext of a prior engagement.' He grinned wickedly. 'I persuaded her to let me see the outfit and then suggested she lay on the poshness of the venue for our meal tonight so that you would wear it.'

Bea felt so embarrassed that Ruth had told him of her deception that she tried to pull away from him, but he resisted and took her into the empty main hall of the house where a welcoming log fire was glowing.

'This way,' he told her, pushing open a door into a darkened room. The lights were switched on as if by magic and, blinking, Bea saw and heard a mass of people singing a chorus of 'Happy Birthday'.

Amongst the sea of faces Bea could make out colleagues from work, friends from church and even some of Ruth's friends.

Bea was so overcome with emotion at all the effort that must have gone into the planning that when she turned to thank her daughter the room swam around her. Liam grasped her arm even tighter.

'Is this all Ruth's work?' she whispered as he led her across the room to a seat between Alicia and Katy.

'Mostly. With a little bit of advice.'

'From you,' she breathed, realisation dawning as to what they'd been talking about all week. They'd obviously been planning all this. But what about the cost?

'How—? Who—?'

'Forget the questions and just enjoy yourself.' She suspected he'd interrupted because he knew what she was about to ask, but she couldn't pursue the matter because Katy was pushing a mound of gaily wrapped parcels across the table to her.

'Goodness! I can't believe all this. And I never suspected for a moment.'

Katy laughed. 'Ruth's been on tenterhooks all day. She was sure someone would let the cat out of the bag, but we were all very good.'

'I don't know where to start.' Bea reached to pick up the nearest package, but Liam stayed her hand. 'Nowhere at the moment, because we're dancing.'

He led her onto the dance floor, past a delighted Ruth who was dancing with a man whose face she recognised but couldn't place.

'Thank you. Thank you,' she mouthed at her daughter, who was looking very pleased with herself, and Bea wondered again about the cost of the evening. Had everyone chipped in or...

The music had changed to a slower beat and Liam pulled her close so that he could rest his cheek on hers. 'Relax and enjoy the evening,' he murmured. 'You can hold the post-mortem with Ruth tomorrow when you're opening all those presents.'

Wondering at him always managing to read her mind, she thought she knew the answer. He was preventing her asking the question because he didn't want her to know he'd financed the entire party.

Time for those questions later. She was going to enjoy the evening. She smiled up at him and as he pulled her even closer she relaxed against the hardness of his muscles.

'That's better,' he told her, nuzzling the top of her hair. She breathed in his musky masculine scent and felt so right there that it was a wrench to drag herself out of his arms when the music stopped.

She didn't know when she had enjoyed an evening more and she couldn't believe the proprietorial behaviour shown by Liam every time anyone else asked her to dance. It made her realise how vulnerable to gossip she would be when Ruth left them alone in the house. That was if she wasn't already!

Ruth joined her and introduced her partner. Of course, it was Dave, one of the theology students, and Debbie was with Ben. Had she been so precoccupied with Liam's presence that she hadn't noticed their friendship developing?

'I enjoyed the service you did,' she told him, and

watched as an expression of obvious pride in her companion spread across Ruth's face.

At the end of the evening Liam offered to drive Bea home so that Ruth could take Debbie and their partners home first.

While Bea thanked everyone for coming and for the unopened presents Liam was carrying out to the boot of his car, Ruth whispered, 'I'll probably have a coffee with Deb before I come on. Is that OK? And I promise I haven't had even a taste of alcohol, Mum.'

Bea grinned. 'I knew you wouldn't have.'

As Liam helped her into the passenger seat of his car, he murmured, 'What a wonderful job you made of bringing up that girl.'

His accolade was the final touch to a wonderful evening that Bea didn't want to end. After she'd helped him indoors with all the tempting packages, she said, 'Coffee, or a nightcap?'

He crossed to where she was standing and wrapped his arms around her. 'All I want is you. You must surely realise that by now.' His lips were warm and dry and did more than emphasise his words as they pressed against hers. A helplessness overwhelmed her as he gently released her and half led, half carried her over to the settee.

Her head nestled against his chest as his arm round her shoulder moved her gently closer, and she knew that, despite her fears, it was what she wanted.

His kiss was much deeper this time, and as their tongues tangled Bea felt his hand move inside the top of her dress and she was powerless to resist. Until she felt his thumb gently circling the very tip of her left breast and knew she was losing control.

Her body tingled with an increasing awareness of

him. She wanted him, loved him so much, but she knew in a moment of clinical detachment that there was no way she could allow him further because she would be the one left alone and hurting when he went away.

She gently removed his hand and murmured, 'I can't, Liam. Ruth will be home soon.'

'She knows how I feel about you,' he murmured. 'We could go to your room. Or mine.'

'It would be the worst thing I could do at this time—set her such a bad example just as she's leaving home.'

He sighed and swore softly at the sound of Ruth's key in the lock. He moved quickly into the kitchen and slowly filled the kettle. Bea guessed he needed a few moments to allow his arousal to subside, and she felt as if her own heart was breaking at his disappointment *and* her own. But she knew it would be much worse if she once allowed him to make love to her.

CHAPTER TEN

DESPITE the late hour, Ruth bounded into the room in her usual energetic way. 'Did you enjoy that, Mum? I know I did.'

'It was fantastic, love. Incredible.' Bea hugged her daughter warmly. 'Thank you so much for planning it. And I never even suspected.'

Liam had returned to the living room, but remained just inside the door.

Ruth grinned at him. 'Liam's been wonderful. I couldn't have done it without his help.'

Bea turned towards him and murmured, with more than a hint of query in her voice, 'I guess I have a great deal to thank you for.'

With an amused lift of his eyebrow he said, 'Post-mortems and present-opening tomorrow. Remember?'

'Today,' said Ruth, laughing. 'But much later, if that's OK by you. I'm bushed and I'm off to bed.'

She kissed her mother goodnight, then after a moment's hesitation kissed Liam on the cheek. 'You don't mind, do you?'

He shook his head and ruffled her hair affectionately, making Bea's heart contract painfully.

He *was* behaving like the father Ruth had never had, and she was clearly revelling in it.

It was a relationship Bea would welcome, if only it could be permanent. But that was wishful thinking when, after January, they would probably never see him again.

When they were again alone Bea felt the tension palpably rise, and to avoid meeting his gaze she plumped up the cushions they had disturbed.

'Bea—' he started, but she interrupted brightly.

'I think I'll go to bed, too. It's been a wonderful evening, but I need my beauty sleep.'

'Bea,' he said again, firmly this time. 'Sit down.'

'I—I can't, Liam.' The temptation was too great. She was finding it increasingly difficult to resist him and she knew from experience where it would end if she didn't. And she couldn't, wouldn't, not with Ruth in the house. In fact, not even when Ruth had left. If she ever slept with a man again, it *had* to be within a committed relationship.

He uttered an exasperated sigh. 'All I was going to suggest was that we talked over a cup of coffee.'

Still clasping the cushion protectively, she stared at him with wide eyes. 'Not tonight, Liam. I'm too tired.' Bewildered by the sensations flooding through her, and under the influence of a little too much to drink, it wasn't the time for serious chat. There was no knowing what she might agree to.

'You still can't trust me,' he uttered despondently.

Tears filled her eyes. 'I can, Liam, and I do. It's myself I can't trust. Goodnight, and thank you for a wonderful evening.'

She threw the cushion onto the nearest chair and fled from the room.

Liam remained motionless. He heard Bea move from the bedroom to the bathroom and back again. Then, when it was all quiet, he switched off the lights and slowly climbed the stairs. To bed, but not to sleep. The knowledge that the first woman he had ever loved sufficiently to make a commitment to was lying alone in the next room to him was almost more than he could bear.

And yet he could understand her wish not to set her daughter a bad example, so he would be patient and wait until Ruth was safely at university. Perhaps once Bea saw her happily settled she might even agree to join him abroad for the year. Because he was sure she loved him and once they were alone together…

His thoughts tailed off into a delicious fantasy of just what they *would* do and eventually, exhausted, he slept.

Bea didn't sleep. It had been a fantastic evening and she knew she had wanted nothing more than for Liam to continue his love-making. But she had to consider first and foremost Ruth and then her own sanity. Because if she had allowed herself to succumb, both would be affected.

Ruth would see him as the father she had never had, only to lose him again, and the pain she herself would feel would be too intense to bear.

How she was going to get through the rest of the weekend she didn't know. Perhaps she could go to the shops with Ruth under the pretext of getting the last few items her daughter needed. And on Sunday they would be at church so, apart from mealtimes, she could avoid being alone in Liam's company.

It didn't work out that way at all. When she eventually did get to sleep, Bea overslept. It was after ten when she slipped down to the kitchen to boil the kettle for coffee and found Liam there with her breakfast almost ready and the coffee brewed.

He poured her a cup. 'Did you sleep well?'

'Like a log,' she lied. 'What about you?'

'Another log. Take that up to bed and I'll bring up your breakfast.'

Aware of the dangers inherent in such a move, Bea's shake of her head was vehement. 'Now I'm up I'll stay, thanks. Mmm—this is very welcome.'

He placed a plate of eggs and bacon in front of her and a rack of fresh toast.

'I—I don't—'

'You need your strength to open all those presents! Ruth's in the bathroom and will be down soon to help.'

'Ruth! Up at this time on a Saturday morning? I don't believe it.'

'A mug of my coffee did the trick.'

Yawning widely, Ruth joined them. 'You've spoilt our surprise, Mum. We were going to bring the prezzies up to your room with breakfast.'

Bea smiled at her foolishness. They wouldn't have been in the bedroom alone after all. 'Sorry about that.' She indicated the cooked breakfast. 'Are you having some?'

'Ugh, no. Coffee's all I want.'

It was lunchtime before Bea had opened and ex-claimed over the last present, and she said quickly to Ruth, 'We need to go shopping for a few last-minute bits and pieces. You'll be packing next Saturday.'

'I'll treat you to lunch first,' Liam told them.

Ruth accepted eagerly for them both, but Bea wasn't happy about it. Every time she'd mentioned the cost of the previous evening he'd dismissed the subject.

She was overruled once again, and they went to the little bistro he'd taken them to before. After a lovely meal, accompanied by Ruth's and Liam's outrageous hilarity, he left them to do their shopping.

Bea immediately demanded to know if Liam had financed the party.

'I'm not allowed to say.'

'It *was* Liam, wasn't it?'

Bea shrugged. 'Does it matter? He wanted to do it because he thinks you're special.'

'Because he's sorry for me more like.'

'Oh! Mum, you're like a terrier. Won't stop worrying until you know every why and wherefore. Well, you'd better not let on that I told you. Both of us wanted you to have a smashing evening. You haven't had many parties over the years.'

'And I suppose you told him that as well?'

'No, but if I had, would it matter?'

Bea gave up. 'I want to go into this secondhand bookshop.'

'What for?'

'One of our patients in hospital. I want to get her a book that's out of print. It was what she was searching for when she fell down the cellar steps.'

Bea didn't find it in the first or the second shop she tried, and was about to give up hope when Ruth suggested a stall in the small covered market.

They could hardly believe it when they found it there, especially when the stallholder told them it had only come in that morning.

They quickly finished the remainder of their shopping and returned home laden.

'A few last-minute bits, eh?' Liam laughed.

The evening she'd been dreading passed pleasantly. Debbie, Dave and Ben came over and they played Scrabble in teams of two. Bea and Liam won easily, so they retired to organise refreshments, leaving the others to enjoy another game.

While Ruth ran her friends home, Bea and Liam cleared up the supper dishes. Bea was at first relieved when Liam made no move to even kiss her, then puzzled and, perversely, by the time she went to bed even a little hurt.

She was even more surprised the next morning when Liam elected to attend the morning service with them.

'I warn you it's a very lively church—lots of participation by the congregation.'

He smiled. 'Fine by me.'

Bea watched him nervously as the service began and then relaxed as she saw him apparently enjoying himself.

On the way home she asked, 'What did you think?'

'Of the service?'

She nodded.

'Certainly my kind of worship. In fact, as Dave and Ben are helping with the evening service, I thought I'd go again. How about you?'

'We'll be there. Ruth'll make sure of that.'

Bea couldn't believe the weekend she had worried about so much had passed off so smoothly, and she guessed that her rebuffs of his offer to talk after the party had been the reason.

But she must have hurt him deeply and she was miserable about it. When she thought of the knocks he'd already suffered in his life, she felt a complete heel, but she didn't know how to make amends without encouraging him into the relationship that she knew would end in disaster.

He had been the perfect gentleman all weekend and, although she knew that wasn't what either of them wanted, she tried to convince herself it was for the best.

As no more cases of Legionnaires' disease had been identified, the workload at the health centre was nearly back to normal, and over coffee on Monday morning Bea asked Liam if he'd heard anything more from Cilla.

He shook his head. 'And not likely to after what her boyfriend did.'

'Let's hope the pills did the trick, then.'

He shrugged. 'We can only hope—I doubt if we'll ever know.'

On Tuesday morning John asked her to keep the following Monday afternoon free as he'd arranged the interviews for a second nurse that day.

During a lull, Bea rang the hospital and discovered that Sharon was still an inpatient. She decided to visit her the following evening and take the book she'd found. She hadn't had time the previous weekend and certainly wouldn't have time during the coming one.

She mentioned Sharon to Liam on Tuesday evening. 'I thought she'd have been home long before this.'

'I expect they feel she needs an eye kept on her for the time being. I gather that there have been problems and she's still completing her radiotherapy. She's had an infection at the fracture site and the skin isn't healing well on her shin—no doubt due to her poor general condition.'

When Bea arrived at the hospital the next evening, she was surprised to find Sharon looking so well and chatting to another patient in the day room. 'Freda's gone home, then?' she asked.

Sharon actually smiled as she nodded. 'But she's been back to see me a couple of times already.'

'How's the radiotherapy going?'

'Better 'n I 'spected. I finish on Friday.'

'That's great.'

'I saw that doctor—you know, the one what found me—at the clinic the other week. His appointment with the oncologist was just before mine. He must be having treatment as well.'

Bea felt her heart flip, then said dismissively, 'I don't think so. I expect he'd asked to see her about one of his patients.' Sharon seemed satisfied with that, and as it had quite possibly been Sharon they'd been discussing, Bea changed the subject by producing the book she had managed to find.

Sharon's eyes lit up. She flicked through it and said, 'This is the one. *Helen's Babies*. Your mother found it, then? It's the kind of book everyone keeps, isn't it? I promise I'll look after it and when I find mine I'll give it you back.'

Bea smiled and said, 'You keep it. I don't want you going down into that cellar again!'

Sharon shuddered. 'I certainly won't do that.'

It was as Bea was leaving the hospital that a niggle of doubt crept through her mind as to what Liam *had* been doing in the oncology department. Doctors usually rang to discuss their patients rather than visit personally, and hadn't Mr Darby seen him at the hospital another day?

Surely there couldn't be anything wrong with him? She tried to laugh off her fears. He looked so healthy and yet why had he taken that Monday off without warning?

She tried to dismiss the notion as ridiculous, but the more she thought about it the more suspicious she became. But when she thought of him visiting the gym three and four times a week, surely it was impossible?

But she couldn't dismiss the idea completely. In fact, she wondered if that been what he'd been going to share with her after her birthday party when she'd refused to listen.

Was that why he'd been so distant since? The thought that it might be something serious made her catch her breath painfully. It couldn't be, surely, not on top of all the other knocks he'd suffered? It wouldn't be fair.

She remembered him disagreeing when she'd said that those families burdened with more than one problem always appeared to be strong enough to cope with them. Was that why? Did he feel he'd already suffered an unfair share?

A painful lurch of her heart left her in no doubt, if she'd ever had any, that she *did* love him. Suddenly she needed to know the truth because if he was ill she wanted to be the one to take care of him. To lovingly nurse him back to health.

Her emotions stirred to a fever pitch, she made up her mind to ask him at the first opportunity, but she was thwarted by him appearing to avoid being alone with her at work, and whenever they were at home Ruth was also present. And bad news like that was something *she* didn't need just before she left for university.

When, late on Friday afternoon, Liam said he wouldn't be home on Friday night or until late Saturday, her imagination began working fiercely overtime. It was all she could do not to blurt out her concern in front of Ruth and Katy.

Although aware that he didn't need to explain his absence, she convinced herself that the fact that he hadn't had to mean it was connected with his health. Was he going into hospital for a biopsy? Or for more treatment? Or…? The alternatives were too horrific to consider.

Ruth clearly thought Bea's preoccupation was due to

nothing more than her leaving for university. 'You'll be fine, Mum. Especially with Liam here.'

She couldn't tell Ruth that it was Liam who was worrying her, especially when at breakfast on Sunday morning he offered to take them with all Ruth's luggage in his borrowed car. 'Just for company on the way back. And it has more boot space.'

Unsure if he was well enough, Bea had reservations, but in the end, for Ruth's sake, she accepted. It could be the opportunity to talk she'd been looking for.

'We'll stop at a place I know in the Cotswolds for a meal before we get there.'

When they left Ruth in her room on campus, with friends she'd made already, Bea brushed away a tear and Liam wrapped an arm around her. 'Bristol's not that far and she'll soon be on the telephone to you, I guarantee.'

She nodded, but remained downcast, suddenly afraid to ask the questions that had been searing her imagination all week.

He seemed aware of her indecision, and when he didn't need his left hand for driving manoeuvres he rested it consolingly on her knee.

When they arrived home, he switched the kettle and settled beside her on the settee.

'Now I have you to myself we have a lot of time to make up.'

'Liam, I—'

'I love you, Bea.'

She froze where she was sitting.

'You can't,' she countered nervously, thoughts of his health uppermost in her mind.

'Why on earth not?' He came slowly towards her

and, grasping the cushion between them, threw it onto the nearest chair.

'I'm the mother of an eighteen-year-old,' she gabbled nervously. 'I'm too old for love.'

'At thirty-seven? Ancient,' he teased. 'Not that it makes one jot of difference. Are only the young allowed to fall in love?'

'No, but—'

The moment I met you I couldn't believe that you hadn't been snapped up long ago, that someone as beautiful and clever and full of life as you are was still there waiting for me. As I got to know you better I realised that for Ruth's sake you've never let men get near enough to fall in love with you.'

'I have plenty of male friends,' she muttered defensively. 'As you must have seen at my party.'

'Acquaintances, colleagues maybe, but—'

'As you are…'

He swept her into his arms. 'Bea, if this is the only way to make my point, so be it.'

He bent his head and his lips met hers with a firm certainty. Her breathing quickened, and when his gently probing tongue invaded the sensitive area behind her lips, she allowed herself to savour the unique taste and feel of him.

When he eventually released her he took both her hands in his and said seriously, 'You must know how I feel about you, Bea, but before I ask you to marry me or even to allow me to make love to you, I *do* have something to tell you.'

'I knew it. You're ill. How ill?'

He frowned, obviously surprised by her outburst. 'I'm not ill now,' he told her gently, 'but I have had testicular cancer and have been waiting for the all-clear before I declared my feelings. I received that reassurance the week before your party and that was what I wanted to tell you that night.'

She raised their clasped hands to her cheeks in anguish. 'Oh, Liam, you must have been bursting to tell someone your good news and I refused to listen because—'

'Because you care about Ruth, and that's right. Six weeks ago you knew nothing about me.'

'Apart from the fact that you're going to Malaysia in February.' She was desolate.

'Which means you believe I'm just on the lookout for someone to pass the time with?'

She nodded hesitantly, but as she was about to speak he silenced her with a finger on her lips. 'I wasn't prepared to declare my love until I knew I wasn't saddling you with a future invalid. Like poor old Mrs Gray.'

'Oh, Liam, I'm—'

'Going to listen this time! Because I want you to have all the facts before I ask you to make a decision.'

'There's no—'

Once again he didn't let her finish. 'I had sperm frozen, Bea, before I had the chemotherapy but, as you know, that's no guarantee of fatherhood.'

After all her fears of the past week, the relief was so great that she burst into tears. 'I love you, Liam, but—'

He tightened his arms around her and gave her a comforting squeeze. 'I love you to distraction, Bea, but it won't be the first disappointment I've had to cope with if you find the fact that I'm not a whole man repulsive. I'll—'

'Don't you ever dare think that, Liam Taylor,' she cried. 'You're more of a man than anyone I've ever met, and you know as well as I do that being sterile doesn't prevent you being the best lover in the world.' She grinned wickedly. 'And there's no risk either! That's got to be a bonus.'

She raised her eyes to search his face and read such an overwhelming love there that she experienced a suffocating clenching of her chest muscles.

He lifted her and carried her up to her bed. She murmured, 'I'm so lucky, Liam. I have Ruth and I'd love a child of yours, but if it's not to be, I can live with that. As long as I have you.'

It was many hours later that she broached the question that was hovering at the back of her mind. 'Do you *have* to go to Malaysia?'

'My contract depended on receiving a clean bill of health and, though John thinks I'm mad, I'm not going to let them down now that I have.'

Bea felt a sudden fear. 'Does John think it'll be too much for you?'

He laughed. 'He's over-protective. I can't deny that the tiredness that followed my treatment lasted longer than I expected, but John won't believe I need to fight it rather than give in to it. That's why he insisted I took that Monday off.'

He held her away from him and searched her face with a tenderness in his expression that made her tears flow again.

'I don't want you to go, Liam. I can't bear the thought of you being so far away for the next year. Anything could happen to you.' She laughed almost hysterically. 'Your life hasn't exactly been incident-free up to now!'

'Come with me, then, and look after me.' He nuzzled her hair, her neck, and nibbled at her earlobe, before trailing kisses down to her shoulder.

'I can't, Liam,' she cried hopelessly. 'Ruth might need me and I wouldn't be there.'

'Did she look as if she was going to need you when you left her? She was already surrounded by friends and Dave's college is only just down the road.'

'But—'

'I told you she thinks you should travel because she appreciates how much you've sacrificed for her.'

'But if she's ill, or—'

He kissed her gently. 'We won't be on the moon. You can be home within a day from most parts of the world and certainly from where I'm going.'

She thought about the near brush he'd had with death, the blows life had already dealt him and his belief that it might help Jenny and Stan if he was abroad, and then she thought of Ruth, already too busy with her new friends to worry about Bea leaving. Suddenly she discovered there was no contest.

Especially when she wouldn't need to go until the New Year when Ruth should be well settled.

'I love you so much, Liam. I *will* go with you, to the ends of the earth if necessary.'

Between his repeated kisses she murmured, 'Liam, what about the health centre? I can't let them down, can I?'

He must have heard the doubt in her voice and reminded her of the interviews the next day. 'John can appoint two new nurses tomorrow, giving them a chance to settle in before you leave. Now, can we return to the task in hand?'

He moved his hands slowly across her abdomen and down the outside of her thighs.

'You certainly know how to persuade a girl,' she murmured huskily.

'I'm glad to hear it.' His fingers crept lightly across, searching for her arousal, 'because one of you really isn't enough for me. I'm hoping you'll agree to us retrieving that sperm and trying for a little one sooner rather than later.'

She kissed him and murmured, 'Can't be too soon for me.' She sat up suddenly and said, 'Talking of fertility, have you heard anything from the Crays since she started her treatment?'

His exasperation was clear as he pulled her back down beside him. 'Don't you *ever* stop thinking about your work? The sooner you leave that health centre the better. I refuse to share our marital bed with your patients!'

She laughed. 'Pity—because I intended to make you my number one patient from now on.'

'Now, that's something I'm ready to agree to.'

MILLS & BOON®

Makes any time special™

Copyright © Harlequin Enterprises Limited 1997
All rights reserved

Mills & Boon publish 29 new titles every month. Select from...

Modern Romance™   Tender Romance™

Sensual Romance™

Medical Romance™   Historical Romance™

MAT2

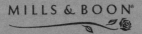

MILLS & BOON®

Medical Romance™

A MOTHER BY NATURE *by Caroline Anderson*

Audley Memorial Hospital

Adam Bradbury is a gifted paediatrician and a devoted father. But he is sure that his inability to have children of his own will push any woman away. But Anna knows that Adam is wrong and she is determined to prove it...

HEART'S COMMAND *by Meredith Webber*

Major Harry Graham had been drafted in to save the outback town of Murrawarra from torrential flood water but he hadn't bargained on Dr Kirsten McPherson's refusal to be evacuated...

A VERY SPECIAL CHILD *by Jennifer Taylor*

Dalverston General Hospital

Nurse Laura Grady knew that her special needs son, Robbie, would always be the centre of her life. Could paediatric registrar Mark Dawson persuade her that he wanted both of them to be the centre of his?

On sale 2nd February 2001

Available at most branches of WH Smith, Tesco, Martins, Borders, Easons, Volume One/James Thin and most good paperback bookshops   0101/03a

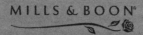

Medical Romance™

THE ELUSIVE DOCTOR *by Abigail Gordon*

Ambitious Dr Nina Lombard did not want to be in the quaint village of Stepping Dearsley! But now that she was working for Dr Robert Carslake, Nina found that she had a reason to stay…

A SURGEON'S REPUTATION *by Lucy Clark*

Dr James Crosby has made his attraction clear to Dr Holly Mayberry but something from his past is holding him back. When James's reputation is put on the line Holly knows she has a chance to win his trust and his heart…

DELIVERING LOVE *by Fiona McArthur*

New Author

Poppy McCrae has always used complementary therapies in her work as a midwife. Paediatrician Jake Sheppard thoroughly disapproves of her methods. Can Poppy persuade Jake to accept her and her beliefs?

On sale 2nd February 2001

Available at most branches of WH Smith, Tesco, Martins, Borders, Easons, Volume One/James Thin and most good paperback bookshops

0101/03b

MILLS & BOON®

0102/98/MB10

THIS TIME...
MARRIAGE

*Three brides get the chance to make
it This Time... Forever.*

**Great value—
3 compelling novels in 1.**

Available from 2nd February 2001

4 FREE
books and a surprise gift!

We would like to take this opportunity to thank you for reading this Mills & Boon® book by offering you the chance to take FOUR more specially selected titles from the Medical Romance™ series absolutely FREE! We're also making this offer to introduce you to the benefits of the Reader Service™—

★ FREE home delivery
★ FREE gifts and competitions
★ FREE monthly Newsletter
★ Exclusive Reader Service discounts
★ Books available before they're in the shops

Accepting these FREE books and gift places you under no obligation to buy, you may cancel at any time, even after receiving your free shipment. Simply complete your details below and return the entire page to the address below. *You don't even need a stamp!*

YES! Please send me 4 free Medical Romance books and a surprise gift. I understand that unless you hear from me, I will receive 6 superb new titles every month for just £2.40 each, postage and packing free. I am under no obligation to purchase any books and may cancel my subscription at any time. The free books and gift will be mine to keep in any case.

M1ZEA

Ms/Mrs/Miss/Mr ....Initials.................................
BLOCK CAPITALS PLEASE

Surname ....

Address ....

....

....Postcode...................................

Send this whole page to:
UK: FREEPOST CN81, Croydon, CR9 3WZ
EIRE: PO Box 4546, Kilcock, County Kildare (stamp required)

Offer valid in UK and Eire only and not available to current Reader Service subscribers to this series. We reserve the right to refuse an application and applicants must be aged 18 years or over. Only one application per household. Terms and prices subject to change without notice. Offer expires 31st July 2001. As a result of this application, you may receive further offers from Harlequin Mills & Boon and other carefully selected companies. If you would prefer not to share in this opportunity please write to The Data Manager at the address above.

Mills & Boon® is a registered trademark owned by Harlequin Mills & Boon Limited.
Medical Romance™ is being used as a trademark.